PASSAG

PASSAGE TO LOVE

AN ELLIS ISLAND STORY

Carolyn Caines

Carolyn Caines

PASSAGE TO LOVE

Copyright © 2011 Carolyn Caines

ALL RIGHTS RESERVED

Carolyn Caines
108 Villa Road
Kelso, WA 98626

Cover photo courtesy of:
http://www.dreamstime.com/free-stock-photo-whole-statue-of-liberty-rimagefree800741-resi3620360

2nd Edition

ISBN: 978-1-105-09909-0

Thomas Juntunen and Reeta (Wayrynen)
on their wedding day, April 6, 1909
Astoria, Oregon

DEDICATION

This book is dedicated to my grandparents, **Reeta and Thomas Juntunen**, whose story inspired me, and whose prayers have followed me in the many years since their passing. Their lives are a legacy for generations to come. I think they both would have dismissed the idea that their story would be important enough to tell. It is.

This book is also dedicated to the memory of their children, **Einer, Leonard, Selma** (my mother), **Arthur,** and **John**, all of whom have now passed on as well.

The Juntunen Family

Back Row L to R: Arthur, Leonard, Einer, John
Front Row: Selma, Thomas, Reeta

ACNOWLEDGEMENTS

I wish to thank my writing instructor, **Dorothy VanWoerkom**, who helped edit and rewrite the first three chapters and who said I must finish this book.

Thanks to my first reader, **Mary Dehnert**, who eagerly awaited each new chapter, spurring me on with her encouragement.

Thanks to many **friends and family members** who have already read this story, insisting that it needed to be published.

I'm especially thankful that **Mom**, **Dad**, and **Uncle John**, each had a chance to read the manuscript and approve of it before their passing.

Contents

Chapter One

PROSPECTS

"That…that boy is a spineless, sniveling, mother's baby!" Reeta fumed. "How could you even think of him? Why must you keep pushing me?" Fighting back tears of disbelief, she dropped the neatly-tied, brown parcel onto the worn table in the center of the room. Speckles of precious brown sugar burst from a ruptured corner of the package.

"Watch what you're doing there, child," Mother chided, quickly retrieving the package. Setting it upright she wasted no time brushing the spilled sugar into her cupped hand before depositing it carefully into a covered crock on the table. She didn't look directly at Reeta, but obviously was not dismissing her either. "You will listen to me, Elsa." began the insistent, lecturing voice.

"Don't call me that," Reeta interrupted. The words came before she could stop them. "Everyone calls me Reeta but you." Under her breath she added, "I hate the name Elsa."

Swiftly turning toward the door, she tried to avoid her mother's hurt expression. Reeta hung her shawl on the nearest peg, hesitating a minute as her fingers smoothed the folds of its serviceable, coarse weave. Deliberately taking a deep breath, she hoped somehow to avoid the inevitable. Why did one thing always lead to another? Now she'd upset her mother instead of gaining her sympathy.

"And why would I give you your dear departed grandmother's name if I didn't want to use it?" Mother asked indignantly. She wiped aside a wisp of gray hair which had only recently invaded the warm brown waves framing her face. Women in her family rarely showed their age, and these silver sentinels had marked a distressing signal.

"The fact is, young lady, you are now eighteen, and not a prospect in sight. Just how many acceptable young men do you think are going to march up to this door and ask for your hand? You can't be so picky, Elsa," she added with exasperation, "or one day you will wake up and discover yourself alone, without a husband or children, like your sister!"

The blunt words found their mark. Reeta whirled around to protest, but her own words caught in her throat at the sight of her older sister. White and trembling, Hanna stood in the doorway from the back room. She must have been there long enough to hear the last remark.

At twenty-six, Hanna was taller than Reeta by several inches, and if not beautiful, at least pleasing to look at. She was skilled in cooking and sewing, and a passing fair scholar and conversationalist. It wasn't her fault the choice of men in the village was so poor, or the men so nearsighted.

Hanna lowered her eyes and quickly disappeared back through the doorway.

If only she would stand up for herself, thought Reeta. But then, she knew Hanna had not chosen things to be as they were. She would gladly have taken a husband; God had not willed it for now.

Reeta glanced in the wood-framed mirror by the coat pegs and inspected her warm, coffee-colored hair, tied in neat braids and looped over the top of her head. Her high forehead was wrinkled with frown lines. She must stop that if she ever hoped to escape the same wrinkles permanently etched in her mother's face.

Purposely relaxing the tension in her face and hopefully in her heart, Reeta turned to the task of supper preparations. She scrubbed the potatoes ruthlessly, whether from frustration or desire for cleanliness she could not tell. Mother already had begun to grind the dark coffee beans. The distinctive bittersweet aroma seemed to have some power to cheer and even ease the tension between them. It wasn't that she tried to have these clashes of will with her mother, they just happened. They were too much alike in many ways, the most obvious: stubbornness.

Hanna eventually appeared from the hallway, joining silently in the tasks which had become nearly a ritual, each participant knowing well their parts. She climbed a short ladder to reach the pole across the rafters that held the week's supply of large, doughnut-shaped loaves of dark rye bread. Carefully removing an especially plump loaf, she carried it to the long table in the center of the room. There she began slicing thick pieces of the black-crusted bread. So deft were her motions, so unemotional the look on her face, that any hurt or offense she felt was well-hidden.

Stoic faces were a portion of life in the small villages and farms around Puolanka. Fiercely independent Finns, like her father, taught their children that only through hard work and perseverance could they make a life for their families. Reeta knew only too well that the whims of nature could be cruel; families had to stick together.

Perhaps Mother was right. Though they irritated each other unendingly, Reeta believed her mother wanted the best for her daughters, at least what she discerned to be the best. Who but God himself could know the truth of the matter?

By the time the stew pot was bubbling with thick slices of beef, fat golden potatoes, and sliced carrots, Mother had begun her discourse on landowners. Reeta knew it by memory.

"You know, girls, it's not an easy life the Good Lord has given us here. He expects your father and me to provide the best future for both of you that we can. That, my daughters, means husbands of the landowning class."

Mother stirred a few grains of salt into the stew as she continued, "We have not struggled all these years to keep our land, only to have you lose that advantage by marrying some poor tenant farmer who cannot keep meat and potatoes on the table."

Here it comes, thought Reeta.

"No land, no future!" Mother preached with righteous zeal. "Love is a thing that will come if the Lord chooses to bless your marriage. And if he chooses not, life is not so bad either."

No need to answer Mother or venture an opinion. Feeling the room grow increasingly stuffy, Reeta excused herself, taking her shawl and retreating outdoors. She headed directly past the sauna and across the west meadow, now empty and stark. It was dressed only in its October stubble, like a man soon to awaken from a long sleep. The chilly afternoon air nipped at her small frame, but Reeta pulled the thin shawl closely around her shoulders. Intending to be gone for a few minutes only, she paid little attention to the sky, portending certain change with the approaching evening.

Coming to the far edge of the meadow, Reeta stepped directly into the woods. It was like taking one step across the threshold of one world into another. Here, the pine trees spread their ancient arms, practically blocking out the sun. But the dim light didn't slow her down. Instead, she quickened her step, ducking under low-hanging branches and avoiding bare tree roots protruding from the hard-packed earth. Darkness hovered in large clouds overhead, but she didn't think of turning back.

There it was, just a few feet ahead: a huge rock, silhouetted against the blue-gray of the sky. Small cracks and crevices served as a stairway along one side, leading up to a perfectly smooth seat along the flat top. Reeta gathered her heavy skirts with one hand and managed the climb in only a few minutes. Resting on the cool seat, she breathed deeply of the crisp air. The view was exhilarating.

Directly beneath her perch, the trees stopped suddenly and a deep valley gaped in a friendly yawn. Small trees and dense shrubbery grew on the steep sides of the cliff. Far below, an almost hidden stream murmured its melancholy song. Sometimes she felt like an intruder in this sacred valley where God and nature communed in a secret tongue. But she did belong. This valley was part of her and had been since childhood. It was her refuge, her confidant.

Reeta set her mind deliberately upon the question at hand, trying to think objectively, without the fetters of emotion. Maybe Mother was right; she should get serious about choosing one of those young men who appeared now and then. Some were friends of her older brothers. They often teased her or pleaded brazenly for her attention, but there was nothing exciting about any of them. It was as if the women in their lives were destined only to be cooks and child-bearers. Not that Reeta didn't want to do those things, but there had to be something more. So much for logic.

Gazing at the sky for a moment, she pressed her palms flat against the smooth stone beneath her, drinking in its silent strength. She dearly loved this land, its rocks and trees, the village and small farms, all of which she could conjure up in her mind by simply closing her eyes and thinking of them. However, Reeta sensed again that something important was missing from the picture. The world was certainly bigger than anything she had seen thus far.

"God," she whispered almost fearfully, "I'm so confused right now. I don't know what to do! Please help me; I know You are there. Why do I keep having this strange feeling? Why can't I be happy and just do what Mother wishes? She does love me." No other words would come, though she sat for a few more minutes, struggling with her wandering emotions.

Suddenly the chill of the coming evening sent a freezing breath from the valley below. Reeta shivered and hurriedly slid from her perch, retracing her steps through the woods to the edge of the meadow. From there she could see the warm orange-glow from the main room's small, square-paned windows. Mother would be worried, and it looked as though Father and her brothers were home already. She quickened her pace, making her way carefully through the meadow, avoiding the many chuck-holes and snags left from last month's harvest.

Chapter Two

FATHER'S OUTBURST

Reeta tried to close the door hastily behind her, but a rush of cold air invaded the warmth of the main room, where dinner preparations were nearly complete. Oddly enough, no one took notice of her entry or her flushed face.

Mother stood with her back to the others, stirring the stew in the ancient pot. After testing to see if the potatoes were done by poking a few gently with a table knife, she climbed up on the small stool to reach the serving dishes from the top shelf. Hanna seemed oblivious to everyone as she set the table with the chipped plates and few lovingly polished utensils that Mother had saved from long ago.

Eli and Andrew, the two eldest brothers, were the only men home as yet. They were intent on some private conversation.

"Yes, I'm certain it was Mr. Rauhala they were talking about," Eli said.

"But their family has lived in Puolanka for generations," Andrew insisted. "It wouldn't be likely he'd sell his land and give up his family home for some uncertain prospects."

"Well, these times have changed more than one man's view," Eli replied. He rolled up his sleeves, grabbed the weathered wooden bucket and poured water into the large basin on the worktable. Water gushed in erratic spurts over the side of the basin as Eli lathered the speckled brown soap and sloshed water over his hairy arms and clean-shaven chin. Eyes closed, he reached for the clean towel from its peg nearby.

Andrew followed, washing with distracted enthusiasm. Reeta had seen that look before. He likely had an idea forming in his mind, but was reluctant to speak.

She watched the slosh of the water and the twitch of his eyebrows as she passed by him. Then she picked up the serving dishes piled high with meat and potatoes in steaming heaps. Carrying them toward the table, she felt one platter slipping from her grasp. Hanna grabbed it before it made an untimely landing. They smiled at each other in relief, not saying a word. Neither of them wished to precipitate one of Mother's lectures on carelessness.

"I guess it's the age of the man that surprises me," Andrew continued, as if there had been no lapse of time. "You'd expect some of the younger men to be drawn to America with all the talk of cheap land, adventure, and seeking your fortune."

"And just who is going to make their fortune in America?" came a grumbling voice from the doorway. Father, Matti, and Aatu had all entered at once, bringing with them a wave of the frigid evening air. "Such talk is foolishness," Father said without waiting for a reply.

"Oh, it's news we heard in the woods today," Eli ventured. "You know Mr. Rauhala."

"That old man?" Father asked in disbelief, hanging up his thick woolen coat and tapping his cane on the braided rug by the door. "Why, he can hardly put in a decent day's work. You're not going to tell me he's thinking of pulling up his roots? It can't be true! You must have heard wrong."

"Oh, it's true all right," Eli said. "You know the Russians conscripted his oldest son. I guess he couldn't abide the thought that the same fate might await his other sons."

A strained silence fell with the last words. Andrew was already seated at the table, which nearly filled the center of the room. Reeta watched Father move with his lopsided gait to the head of the table. Rubbing his now almost entirely white beard with a work-worn hand, he looked upon each of his sons in turn while they seated themselves.

Eli, the eldest, was a tall, strapping young man of twenty-four, only recently sweet on little Saara Riihimaki. Andrew, twenty-three, was shorter and of a stocky build, like Mother's side of the family. It was 1905, and how either of them had escaped the heavy Russian conscription was a mystery for which only God could be thanked.

Aatu had just turned seventeen. Mother babied him outrageously because of his long illness which had left him with a pale complexion and sporadic coughing fits. Then there was faithful Matti, who at thirteen was Father's right-hand man. Reeta thought he probably knew more about running the farm than any of the older boys.

Suddenly, Father's fists tightened and Reeta could see the blood vessels pulsing in his temples. When he finally blurted out the words, all eyes were fixed in his direction.

"This is our land. We own it!" he wailed like an animal caught in a trap. "No despicable, vodka-drinking Russian can take it away from us. Anyone who dares to speak a word of that vulgar language in this house...God curse him!"

His words sent a chill through Reeta. She vividly remembered just a few years ago when she had come home from school announcing that Miss Oksanen was going to be teaching them Russian. She had known that her father was opposed to the Russians, but only then did she find how great his passion on the subject was. He had stormed into the small, one-room school the next morning and berated the teacher in front of all the children.

"You are paid, Miss Oksanen, to train our children to read and write, to cipher, to use their hands in diligent and useful labor, and to respect their parents and the Christian faith." Father's face had been flushed with anger as he continued, "But you will not teach my children one syllable of that...that tongue of the enemy of our freedom!"

Miss Oksanen had been kind, even understanding. Ushering Father toward the door, she admitted there was little anyone could do about the edict in general. However, the Wayrynen children had been excused thereafter from Russian language classes.

Now Reeta sat down at her place beside Hanna and Matti on one side of the table. Eli, Andrew, and Aatu were seated on the bench across from them, and Father still stood at the head of the table, his fists clenched, prepared for battle. Only when Mother calmly took her seat at the opposite end of the table did he begin to relax. Looking once more at his family, he rested his work-worn hands on the table and bowed his head. Then everyone followed his move, all heads bowed and hands folded.

"Father in heaven," he began, "be merciful to us, Your children. We thank You for Your blessings and this food we are about to eat."

Usually his prayers at meals were quite brief, but now there was a hesitation, and Reeta opened her eyes to see what was happening. She saw him wipe away a tear that had escaped down his cheek. Quickly she closed her eyes, and he continued. "Lord, we ask Your blessing on our home and land. May we enjoy the freedom of heart and mind that only You can bring. Amen."

"Amen," they added softly in unison. Then lifting their heads respectfully, they awaited the signal to begin. Father sat down, heaving a sigh. It was Mother who reached for the first dish. In a few moments, the clink of spoons against dishes and mundane conversation had all but blocked out the earlier tenseness. Reeta relaxed. Mother's stew, the bread spread thick with fresh-churned butter, and the rich, black coffee, which she had learned to sip as a small child. Yes, this was home. These things are a balm for any trouble in the world, she thought.

"Aatu don't gulp your food so!" Mother reprimanded. "You know it only makes you cough."

Seemingly on cue, Aatu began one of those brief fits of coughing no one paid much attention to anymore. *If only he would get some color in his cheeks,* Reeta thought, glancing at him and noting his sallow complexion. But then, she couldn't remember his ever being any different than he was at this very moment.

An unexpected knocking at the door sent Reeta scurrying. She undid the latch and Thomas Juntunen blew in with the next gust of cold air.

Chapter Three

THOMAS

Windblown and evidently flustered by the sight of the family still seated at the table, Thomas stood inside the door. With scarcely a look at Reeta, he removed his knit cap and directed a nod toward the family.

"I'm sorry to be interrupting your meal," Thomas apologized. "Perhaps I should come back later."

Mother glared across the room. It was that look she gave anyone who upset the family routine or dared to cross the inexplicable social barrier of the landowners.

"You may wait, if you wish," she said condescendingly. She was clearly unimpressed with this young man, choosing to ignore him rather than interrupt her meal.

If it had been Mother's unwelcome stare, or his own self-consciousness, Reeta had little notion, but feeling Thomas' predicament, she tried to smooth over the situation.

"We're nearly finished, Thomas." she consoled. "You're always welcome. Here, let me have your coat."

At her reassuring smile, Thomas removed his worn coat, handing it to her after carefully removing an envelope from one pocket.

Eli greeted him between mouthfuls. "Hey, Thomas! Good to see you."

"Ya," Thomas acknowledged.

But it was Andrew who got to his feet and ushered him to a seat near the fireplace. Turning to Reeta, Andrew shook his head in mock exasperation. "Aren't you going to get our guest some coffee?"

Remembering herself, Reeta went directly to the shelves near the sink and reached for an unchipped cup. Carrying it to the table, she filled the cup with the thick, brown brew. She was aware that Mother was sizing up the situation uncomfortably. Ignoring her, Reeta returned to the fireplace, placing the cup carefully in Thomas' cold hands.

He said merely, "Thank you, Reeta," pausing ever so slightly upon the last word. Something about the way he said her name sparked her interest.

Thomas had been in their home many times with either Eli or Andrew. Her brothers had grown up knowing him, and they didn't let Mother's social distinctions bother them when it came to choosing their friends. Reeta had seen him at school and with the young men at church services, though she had never really noticed him in particular before now.

Considering physical appearance, Thomas had nothing special that would catch the eye of many girls, she supposed. He was only slightly taller than Reeta, perhaps five-foot-three. In a land of tall lumbermen, he was no match, but his frame was filled-out with muscles earned by many days of hard work in the woods, along with keeping up the small tenement farm his parents worked, on the south side of the village. His bushy, soft brown moustache twitched nervously, as he sipped a little coffee. Then he unconsciously smoothed back his hair, revealing a wide forehead now creased in thought.

She must have been staring at him far too long, because he began fidgeting with the cup in his wide, stubby fingers, and Mother appeared at her side, grabbing her by the elbow.

She directed Reeta across the room with a persuasive motion. "Here," she ordered, "take the dishes and scrape them, while I heat up the water."

Reeta reluctantly headed for the table. Hanna had already disappeared, and Father was putting on his jacket and boots. Matti followed his example, bundling up against the cold. With a nod toward Thomas, Father was out the door. The last chores of the day waited for no one, so Matti and Aatu rushed by also, with barely an audible, "Hello, Thomas." Eli and Andrew were exempt from these chores on the days they worked in the woods.

Having finished with his meal, Eli greeted Thomas with a friendly slap on the back. "Well, Thomas, you're looking good. Say, was that Greta I saw you talking to last week? She's quite some girl." Eli chuckled and hooted at his own joke. Greta was infamous for trying to snag one of the village young men.

Playfully, Thomas jabbed Eli in the ribs, informing him with a smile, "Why Eli, she was asking about *you*."

"I wonder what poor creature that girl will finally catch." Andrew joined in. "Anyway, what's this you've got, Thomas?"

Reeta went about her chores, scraping the plates and carrying them to the work table. While she waited for the water to be heated, she tried to listen in on the conversation, but Mother sent her to put away a stack of freshly ironed clothes that had been hanging on a hook near the fire.

Carelessly Reeta stashed the clothes in a heap. She'd pay for this later, but right now, she had to know what Thomas and her brothers were talking about. The voices from the main room were rising in an excited pitch, and Reeta crept slowly toward the doorway, hoping to catch some of what they were saying.

"The letter just arrived today," came Thomas' husky voice. "Veerus wrote all about America, and I knew you would want to read this, too."

Straining to hear, Reeta leaned a little closer to the doorway. Then she lost her balance, and it was too late to regain a steady footing. In a few seconds, which seemed agonizingly longer to her, she found herself lying unceremoniously, arms flung wide across the floor. Eli was helping her to her feet, with Andrew and Thomas gawking.

"Oh-h-h, I must have tripped," she said with a groan. Her palms were red, but she was otherwise unharmed. She hoped they didn't notice her equally red face.

Looking directly at her, Thomas' eyes held a certain glint of amusement, but his words were sincere. "Have you ever seen one of these American stamps, Reeta? Come, have a look. "

She moved toward him, her pride still injured, not letting herself enjoy the attention. Silently she peered at the postage stamp with its strange inscription and postmark. "Where is this place...Stella?" she finally ventured.

"It's not much more than a postal station and store right on the Washington shore of the Columbia River. You've heard of Washington?" Thomas asked.

She thought she knew where that was, but geography hadn't been her best subject, so she only nodded vaguely.

Thomas opened the envelope. Inside was a brief letter from his brother, Veerus, and a pamphlet entitled <u>The Evergreen State.</u>

"Look at this," Thomas said, handing the pamphlet to Eli. "Can you imagine a place with large, snow-capped mountains, thousands and thousands of acres of forest, dairy and meat farming, and land waiting to be taken?"

"It says here that they are looking for 'brave young men and women to take up a new adventure in the marvelous American wilderness,' " Eli quoted.

"Doesn't it sound like *The Kalevala*?" Andrew added. "I can just see the hero looking over his beloved country."

"I don't know about poetry and such," Eli said, "but it sounds like Finland, all right. Only bigger, and richer, and without the problems we have here."

Reeta was lost in thoughts of the epic poem. The hero was strong and brave, never fearful of a new adventure. That would be her idea of a real man. He would lead his love safely through the wild land, defending her from danger. No difficulty would be too great to bear as long as he remained by her side. Her dreams were interrupted when she heard Thomas' final words.

"Well, I think it's fine for the menfolk," he admitted, "but I'd never take a wife into that wilderness until I'd made my fortune and had a decent home for her."

A sharp call from the back room interrupted the conversation. "Reeta!" It was her mother's voice.

Without looking up, Reeta turned, slowly walking toward the doorway. The men continued their excited discussion; this time she wasn't listening. She knew what her mother was angry about, but that wasn't what caused a sick feeling of frustration and disappointment welling up inside her.

How silly of Thomas to think a woman can't endure a little hardship, she thought. Who will be waiting for him if he goes to America? Why does it matter what Thomas thinks, anyway?

Chapter Four

PUOLANKA

Puolanka was buzzing with excitement unlike anything Reeta or Hanna had seen since the days of the Russian conscription. Bits of conversation floated through the early morning air, teasing their curiosity.

"Look at him!" boasted a young man holding out a photograph for his friend to admire. "He's wearing a new suit and fancy shoes. See that expression on his face? He never looked as happy when he lived here."

"It must be a rich land, indeed," his friend said, relishing each detail of the picture.

An old man asked his companion, "Who do you suppose will be the next to go?"

"I heard Rudy say that his uncle is leaving in the spring," was the reply.

"It's so big that you could travel for months and never get to the other side," a little girl explained to her audience of several smaller children. She stretched out her arms wide, like thin spider legs, while they stared with their mouths hanging open.

Reeta and Hanna nodded to a few people they knew, but said little, walking slowly toward the store. They had been sent to collect any mail for the week and to pick up the items on Mother's carefully-written list. Mother usually accompanied them on such trips. Today, however, the swelling and pain in her joints had been too much for her. She had excused herself, asking Matti and Aatu to heat up the sauna, the cure-all for most ailments.

The village itself wasn't much more than a few shops and buildings along one main street. The general store, which housed a postal station as well, occupied a prominent spot beside the public bathhouse and across from the town hall. Sitting at the end of the street was the Lutheran church, guardian-observer of their activities. Pointing toward heaven, its steeple reached high above the everyday business of life.

Groups of villagers deep in discussion gestured toward placards bearing bold red-and-black letters, posted in front of the store. Reeta would have stopped to find out what it was all about, but Hanna pulled her into the store.

"Come along, Reeta," she said very practically. "We've got to get these things and be back in time to help mother with supper."

"Aren't you the least little bit interested in all the talk out there?" Reeta whispered, peering through the store window. "Don't you want to know what's going on in the world?"

"Reeta Wayrynen, you are impossible!" Hanna rebuked, taking out the neatly folded paper containing their needs. She immediately began to gather the items, carefully weighing their quality and price.

Reeta, however, couldn't concentrate on such mundane matters. "I'll go check on the mail," she offered.

"Ya, fine. Just don't be too long," Hanna warned as she turned back to examine the display of needles perfectly arranged in shiny rows by size inside the glass case.

Walking around displays of material, tools, and dry goods, Reeta worked her way to the small window near the back of the store. The window had bars across it, except for the bottom handbreadth, just enough space to slide thin packages and letters underneath. No one had quite figured out the actual use of those bars, except maybe to make Mr. Moilanen feel more important.

"Well, hello there, Miss Wayrynen," Mr. Moilanen greeted her. He readjusted his small, round spectacles to get a better look. His forehead formed rows of wrinkles beneath the shiny domed top. "My, aren't you looking nice today? And how is your mother?"

Reeta fidgeted under the weight of the compliment. "Mother is hurting a little...her joints, you know. She wasn't quite up to the walk."

"Know what you mean, know what you mean," Mr. Moilanen repeated. "Must be that a change in the weather is coming soon. My knee's been acting up a mite, too."

"Any mail for us?" Reeta asked, trying not to interrupt his explanation, but hoping to move things along.

"Let's see here," he said, turning over several letters and looking under another pile. If there were a system to sorting the mail, it didn't really matter to Mr. Moilanen as long as he knew where everything was. "Now I saw something right here. Just a minute...Yes," he said, sliding an envelope under the bars.

It was addressed to Eli Wayrynen, the postmark bearing the name of the port city to the west, Oulu. *Who would be writing her brother from there?* Reeta mused to herself. "Thanks, Mr. Moilanen," she said politely. "I hope your knee gets better." She turned, wandering toward the front of the store where Hanna had nearly completed her purchases.

"Any mail?" Hanna asked while she began gathering up the bundles on the counter.

"Just one letter for Eli. I don't recognize the handwriting. From Oulu." Reeta took some of the bundles from Hanna and they started for the door.

At the front of the store a few villagers were caught up in an argument about emigration, and no one offered to open the door. Reeta grabbed the handle. Her packages, balanced in her arms, were sufficiently blocking her vision so that when she stepped outside, she didn't see him coming.

He wasn't looking where he was going either. Packages flew out of her hands to the rough plank walkway, while Reeta fought to keep her balance.

"I'm sorry!" he immediately apologized, catching her arm in his firm grip. "It was entirely my fault. Here, let me help you."

They both bent over to retrieve the packages, and only then did Reeta realize that it was Thomas. She looked into his eyes for a moment, large soft gray eyes that seemed to look into her soul. The feeling was disconcerting. She stood up at once, collecting her bundles and her composure at the same time.

Hearing hearty laughter, she looked behind Thomas. Jake was thoroughly enjoying the situation. There was no mistaking the one for the other after first glance. Thomas and Jake both had the same build, sandy brown hair, and high foreheads, but everything else about them denied their similarity. Thomas was courteous and always a gentleman, while Jake wore a constant smirk across his lips, as though he considered himself smarter than anyone else. How any twin brothers could be so alike, yet so different at the same time, was beyond her comprehension.

"Reeta, I swear!" Jake said, trying to control his laughter. "It's so nice to bump into you and your lovely sister today."

Hanna gave him a stare that would have stopped lesser scoundrels, but Jake was in his element.

"Say, maybe I could interest you ladies in a little cruise to America?" he said, waving at one of the placards. "Which sailing date would you prefer? Thomas, here, could be your guide through the wilderness. Couldn't you now?"

"Enough, Jake," Thomas warned.

"No harm done, brother," Jake said. "Just joking around, you know."

That doesn't sound like an apology, Reeta thought.

"It's just that the whole country is going crazy," Jake lamented, directing his remarks toward the sisters. "Tell me what's so bad about our life here that my own brothers have to go thousands of miles away. They'll never come back, you know."

Shivers of apprehension crawled up her spine, but Reeta also felt a new emotion. Could she perhaps be envious of the adventurers? She wondered.

"It's not a decision anyone makes lightly," Thomas answered. Then, looking more at Reeta than anyone else, he added, "The gain surely would be worth the loss, if God's blessing were in the adventure."

Reeta looked away so he wouldn't see the mist in her eyes. She hated herself for crying so easily. It's not like this had anything to do with her family.

Hanna interrupted the conversation. "We really must be getting home, Reeta."

"Yes, of course," she replied. "Goodbye." She nodded toward the brothers. Thomas mumbled something she didn't quite hear, while Jake doffed his hat, making a pompous bow for their benefit.

Reeta and Hanna walked home without speaking. The only sounds were the steady rhythm of their shoes thumping against the hard earth and the rustle of the pines swaying in the chilling north wind. The picture of Thomas' gray eyes searching her soul haunted Reeta. What had he seen, she wondered, and what did he want to know?

Chapter Five

ELI'S LETTER

Soon Eli appeared, having finished his morning's work. Reeta immediately retrieved the letter from Oulu out of her apron pocket. Neither Eli nor anyone else in the family received letters frequently, but several had arrived for him in the past few months.

"Here's another letter for you," Reeta said, holding it out to him. "Who's in Oulu?"

The question was simple enough, asked in a casual way, but Eli only frowned at her, withdrawing to the other side of the room to read the letter.

She watched him sitting in the carved rocking chair, the noonday sun casting its speckled light across his lap. He leaned over the letter, his shoulders hunched and weary from the morning's work.

Suddenly he straightened up in the chair, his eyes darting rapidly across the letter again and again. Reeta was about to venture another question when Andrew came striding in, throwing his coat on the hook.

"And what has my little sister been up to?" he asked cheerfully, giving her a pat on the head.

"Hanna and I went to the store for a few things, and Eli got another mysterious letter."

She was about to ask Andrew what he knew about the letters when Eli came to life, bounding across the room. Pushing Andrew out the door, he slammed it behind them both.

"Whatever was all that banging about?" Mother scolded, rushing in from the back room. She placed her fists on her hips, scowling at Reeta, who now was the only one standing in the middle of the room.

"I don't know," she answered, genuinely bewildered. "Eli and Andrew have some secret they're not telling, I guess."

"We'll see about that," Mother said, going back to her work and grumbling to herself all the way.

When the sun was directly overhead, Father was seated in his place at the dinner table. He never needed to be called and hastened to scold anyone who should come in late. Since there was no work in the woods, everyone was home. Mother snatched the opportunity.

"Tell us about your letter, Eli," she said, not making a suggestion, but clearly expecting compliance.

Squirming uncomfortably, Eli seemed unwilling to speak.

"Yes, do," Father added. "Your mother says it must be something special the way you two boys have been carrying on." He held his fork in mid-air, waiting for him to begin.

Eli gave a questioning look at Andrew. Andrew nodded his head, looking about the table with a silly grin of anticipation, or was it nervousness? Before venturing an explanation, Eli swallowed a mouthful of dry bread and drank a long draught of warm milk.

"You see, Andrew and I...we have some news," he said nervously, turning the empty mug around and around between his fingers. "We've decided to go to America."

The words dropped like a heavy curtain around the table. Reeta didn't dare look up from her plate, but sat waiting for what would come next.

Taking a deep breath, Eli continued slowly at first, then with gathering momentum. "There is more land than you can imagine, for sale cheaply, too. We've received word that jobs are waiting for us in a logging camp in Washington. It's near a large Finnish settlement. Many of the settlers have come from right here in Puolanka. You know Thomas Juntunen's brother, Veerus? He's there, and..."

Eli stopped talking, aware that all eyes were on him, Father registering disbelief, and Mother staring in horror. His resolve began to falter.

"We all know that America is the land of opportunity," Andrew said, taking up the well-rehearsed defense, even daring to look his father in the eyes. "Father, you've often said yourself that the land is our future, but not without freedom."

"The land is here, in Finland!" Father corrected, his face quivering with rage. "And we have fought for many generations to keep our independence. You would take your family's heritage so lightly?" He glared at Andrew in disbelief.

"No, you misunderstand me," Andrew protested. He looked to Eli for support.

"Father, you know how many acres we own and how hard it is to make ends meet for our family as it is," Eli reasoned. "What will happen when we have families of our own? What future will our children have? Surely you can see that we are having the life squeezed out of us here."

Father couldn't speak, but Mother found her voice. "You are ungrateful children!" she blurted. "The very idea of going off adventuring! That's what it is, isn't it? The adventure? The excitement? It would wear off soon enough, and then you'd wake up and find yourself stranded on the other side of the world. What's a mother to do?" she wailed in despair, throwing her apron up over her head. That gesture was Mother's sign that she was done speaking. No more to be said.

Reeta had been watching the whole scene in silent confusion. She felt somehow detached from what was going on, as if the people talking were strangers, not her own family. She didn't know how to feel; there was no feeling except perhaps amazement and a sense of being cut apart. Someone had taken a large pair of scissors and had begun cutting the family into separate pieces, Mother and Father in this piece, Eli and Andrew in that piece. And what of the rest of them?

Mother sat stone still until everyone had gotten up from the table. Only then did she remove the embroidered, white apron from her bowed head. Judging by the lack of color in her face, she might well have seen a ghost. Mother always stood her ground, but never pouted for long. She found hard work a welcome relief for tension. Taking a serving dish in each hand, she ordered, "You girls run along and find something else to do. I'll clean up."

That was all the excuse Reeta needed. While Hanna resolutely began to attack the pile of mending overflowing from the basket by the rocker, Reeta quietly put on her long, brown coat, making an escape for the woods. It had been raining during dinner, but now the sun had broken through. Drops of water glistened in rainbow colors, hanging from tree branches and sturdy, blue-green blades of grass.

She didn't hurry along the path this time. Mother would be occupied with other thoughts, and Reeta needed to do some thinking of her own. It must have been Thomas who started all this talk about going to America, she concluded. Perhaps it wasn't fair to blame him entirely. America was all that the people in the village could talk about lately. But Thomas must have persuaded Eli. Why did he keep coming to haunt her? She was beginning to dislike him in a way, and yet she felt strangely drawn into the adventure also.

Preoccupied with her thoughts, Reeta had almost come to the large rock by the cliff before she noticed the figure standing directly in the pathway. A man was leaning against a tree, his back toward her.

For a moment she thought she must be dreaming. The mist from the valley was lifting, and sunlight filtered through the pine branches, casting a dream-like illusion over the place. She stood perfectly still, not daring to breathe, lest the vision escape her. She imagined the young man must be waiting to meet his love, and she had stumbled upon the scene at just the moment before they would see each other.

He was real. He sighed, moving his shoulders ever so slightly, and then tilting his head to listen for some sound in the woods. Startled, she stepped back, snapping a twig underfoot. He turned around in time to catch her staring.

Chapter Six

MEETING IN THE WOODS

He stood up straight, smiling as if he were not at all surprised to see her, as if he had been waiting for her. Reeta, however, had been caught off guard. Her dream had suddenly come to life, and she felt her heart beating wildly.

"Reeta," he said, taking a few steps in her direction, "at last you've come. I was hoping you would be here today."

"Thomas Juntunen, you frightened me so!" Reeta scolded.

Taking another step toward her, he removed his hat and apologized. "I didn't mean to. It's just that I needed to talk to you."

"And how did you know that I might be here? Who told you about this place?" she questioned him suspiciously.

"No one," he protested, trying to explain his presence. "I didn't mean to spy on you, but I took this short-cut one day after visiting your brothers. You've worn quite a path through the woods," Thomas said, smiling now and pointing to the obvious trail behind her. "I followed it and found you sitting up there on the rock."

"I've never seen anyone in this place," Reeta said, as much to herself as to Thomas.

"Oh, I haven't told a soul about it, not even your brothers," he tried to reassure her. "You looked quite deep in thought when I saw you. I felt foolish and couldn't let you know I had found your secret place, so I slipped back into the woods." Thomas hung his head like a schoolboy caught peeking at a test.

"I guess there's no harm done," Reeta admitted. She took a step closer and stood with her hands clasped behind her back, wondering what to do next. Then a thought occurred to her. "Have you ever seen the view from up there? Come on, I'll show you the way to climb up."

Reeta pulled at his coat sleeve, and in a moment they were laughing and racing up the little, jagged steps to the top. They sat down breathlessly, staring in wonder at the peaceful scene below. The valley sparkled with diamond-like raindrops clinging to the thin, green fingers of the pines.

After a few minutes, it was Thomas who broke the silence. He blurted out the words. "Reeta, I've come to ask your advice, you being a woman and all."

She stared at him incredulously, knowing full-well they had barely spoken a handful of words to each other...ever. Surely some intolerable desperation had driven him to seek her out.

"I want to ask," he said, hesitating to stare intently into the valley for a moment, "to ask someone I've chosen, if she will be my wife." Having unburdened himself, he dared to peek at her from the corner of his eyes.

"You want my advice?" Reeta managed to whisper, a sick feeling suddenly overwhelming her. It was as if she had reached out for a branch on the cliff's edge, and it had disappeared, leaving her hanging precariously, ready to fall into the ravine. She realized that she was jealous. In some way she had come to care about him, too late.

Thomas interrupted her thoughts. "Look at me, Reeta."

Slowly she lifted her eyes toward his, not wanting to see the look of one pining with love, for someone else. Had she imagined somehow that he might have been interested in her? She could think of no advice to offer him. "Thomas, I don't know much about this sort of thing," she began to protest.

"Wait. Hear me out," he insisted. "I'm going to America in the spring with Eli and Andrew. I suppose they told you?"

"No, not exactly. They did break the news about their plans to everyone at dinner today," Reeta said. "Mother and Father took it pretty hard. It's so far away, Thomas."

"I know." He paused, evidently hunting for the right words. "It will be a rough life for a while. We'll be working in the logging camp to earn money, but one day I will have enough for my own land, my own farm. It may be a long wait, but do you think the woman I have chosen...do you think she'd wait for me?"

Reeta's head was spinning. Disappointment and reason were struggling against each other, putting her quite off-balance. "Thomas, how could I know?" she replied, turning her eyes from his. She felt sick.

"Reeta, please," Thomas begged, impulsively taking her hands in his rough, work-worn hands.

Amazed, she looked up and was caught in the spell of his searching eyes. "I fear I've said this all wrong," he apologized, a painful expression passing over his face. "It's you, Reeta. Could *you* find it in your heart to wait for me?"

At first she didn't comprehend. Then, slowly the truth of what he had said settled over her mind. She saw him clearly for the first time. It wasn't someone else; Thomas wanted her! Relief, excitement, and an equal amount of confusion tumbled through her heart. "Oh, Thomas! There's so much to consider," Reeta answered slowly. She tried to pull her hands away, but he held them firmly.

I know I'm rushing you, Reeta," he said, "but I need to know if you care for me at all. If you say you will not have me, I must go to America broken-hearted. There is no one to take your place. I don't have much to offer, but you know me, Reeta. I'll work hard to provide for you the best I can. You will have a good home and never want for food and clothing." Thomas stumbled over the next words. "And...and I will love you always. Just give me a little hope."

Reeta stared at Thomas, not knowing how to answer. If feelings were the criterion for love, she had them now. Love must be the tingling sensation, the rapid heartbeat, the sweaty hands, or the desire to stay in this spot forever with him. If love were loyalty and faithfulness, she had no doubt that Thomas could love her, but could she love him that way? Mother said marriage had little to do with love, but Reeta wanted it.

Thomas searched for some sign from her, some ray of hope. Reeta began shivering, either from emotion or the now chilly air.

"Here, let's get down from this rock and away from the wind," Thomas said, pulling her to her feet and helping her climb down the side.

She didn't need his help, but it was a nice feeling--to be cared for. Was that part of love, too? When they reached the shelter of the pine trees nearby, Reeta still had not found the words to express her confusion.

Taking her silence as a negative reply, Thomas said, "I understand, Reeta. I know I must sound crazy. I won't bother you again. Maybe you will change your mind someday." He turned his back to her and began walking away.

"No, wait!" Reeta called.

He was there in a moment. With one look into her eyes, he wrapped her in his gentle bear-like arms, holding her close to his heart.

"Thomas," she said, pushing herself away just far enough to see his face. "I'm afraid I just don't know about love. I do have feelings for you, and I do care about you. Is that enough for now?"

"I will live on those words," he whispered in her hair.

For a few minutes they stood, frozen in time, not wanting to break the spell. Reeta felt like crying and laughing, while at the same time, a wild new aching gnawed inside her, yearning to be fulfilled.

Thomas was the one who pulled away this time. He gently took her hand, and they began walking back through the woods. Coming to the edge of the field, Reeta remembered the events of the morning and stopped him in the shadow of the pines.

"You can't go with me now," she warned.

"I'm not afraid of them," he protested. "Are you?"

"It's not that," she said. "Too much has happened in one day. Mother and Father need time to get used to the idea of the boys leaving, and I don't want to upset them anymore." She looked into his eyes, hoping to see some understanding.

"Of course," Thomas said, realizing his hastiness. "I'll pray your mother can come to like me even a little. I'm a patient man, Reeta; I can wait. Anything good in this life is worth working and waiting for. I'll see you tomorrow at church." With that, he leaned over, placed a gentle kiss on her forehead, and made his way through the trees along the edge of the field.

Reeta stared after Thomas until he disappeared. Heaving a sigh, she started directly across the field toward the house. If it were meant to be, it would work out somehow. *God, let it be!* she prayed. A dark cloud cast its shadow in her path as she began to run for the shelter of the house.

Chapter Seven

SUNDAY DREAMS

That night Reeta lay on her straw-filled mattress, alternately sleeping and waking to the whine of the wind or the creaking of the house. She entertained a thousand images darting in and out of her imagination: familiar faces, strangers, places she had never been, and indiscernible voices.

Exhausted, Reeta lifted her head and looked out the window through red-veined eyes. Dawn was only a few hours away, so she tried again to clear her mind. Finally, sheer weariness overtook her, once more carrying her into a fitful sleep.

There was Thomas, her smiling young hero, come to carry her away to an adventure across the ocean. She wondered at the brilliance of his smile and the watery gray pools of his eyes, colored mysteriously as only a dream could. He reached for her. She could feel his warm hand touching her cheek. Then he was gone, dissolving into little flecks of nothingness.

In his place stood a plain, young farmer beckoning her to come with him. They walked down a pathway clouded with dust to an ordinary-looking cottage, not unlike many she often passed on the way to Puolanka. She followed him inside, turning around in disgust at the sight of dirt and filth in every corner. From the darkness, at least a dozen, scrawny, grimy-faced children ran to her, clinging to her skirt. She pulled back trying to shake them off. Then, as quickly as they had appeared, they too vanished.

Reeta fought to regain consciousness, but a black fog, having a power of its own, enveloped her mind. Two people appeared in the blackness, still too far away to make out. They were coming toward her, an old couple with crinkled faces and pleading eyes.

Closer now, Reeta realized they were her parents, but older, sadder looking. Their feeble hands reached out, holding her so she couldn't leave. She awoke trembling, her body drenched with perspiration.

Hanna was at her side, smoothing back the damp locks of hair from her forehead. "Reeta, are you all right? You've been moaning and tossing about," she whispered earnestly.

She sat up, staring at Hanna in the near-darkness, only the dim moonlight sending silver shadows through the window. "Oh, it was an awful dream!" she exclaimed softly, reaching out to Hanna for assurance.

"Can you tell me about it?" Hanna asked, holding her still-trembling hand.

"No...No! I'll be fine now," Reeta answered, lying back down on the mattress. She patted Hanna's hand, hoping to placate her a little. "Go back to bed. Really, I'm all right."

Hanna moved quietly across the room, but Reeta was wide-awake now. Slowly the dawn came, and with it, a new resolve.

Reeta was the first one dressed. She busied herself with breakfast preparations. Today was Sunday, and that meant a change from the usual hot cereal, bread, and coffee. There would be fried eggs, braided pulla sweetbread, and white "squeaky" cheese, so named because of the squeaky sound it makes when chewed. Each task, easily completed by force of habit, today bore a new interest. Even the four rough-hewn walls of the main room appeared different, something to memorize, each detail to be firmly set in her mind.

Mother woke with the pain and soreness in her joints not even allowing her to get up from her bed without help. Some of the dark moodiness of the previous day had worn away, but no one spoke much during breakfast. A "Pass the butter," or "More coffee?" was the extent of the conversation.

"I can't get these old things to cooperate at all," Mother said, slapping an offending leg. "Here, Reeta, help me back to my bed."

Obediently Reeta offered her arm, guiding her mother slowly to the double bed in the corner of the back room.

When at last she was settled under the warm coverlets and propped up with several pillows, she gazed at Reeta sadly. "At least I have my girls to give me comfort yet awhile. What's a mother to do?"

Reeta shivered involuntarily, remembering the image from her dream.

"We're ready to go!" Aatu called from the front door.

For a moment Reeta stared at her mother, wondering what she would do if she knew about Thomas.

"Don't worry about me, child. Run along now." Mother waved her away with a hand and closed her eyes. "I didn't sleep well last night."

Reeta quickly put on her coat, buttoning it all the way, and added dark green woolen mittens with a matching cap. Staring into the small mirror, she noted the way the cap brought out the green in her hazel eyes.

"Reeta, are you coming?" came a shout from outside.

"I'm ready!" she called, firmly pulling the door closed and stepping down off the porch.

Father held the reins while the chocolate-brown mare pawed the ground, anxious to be off. Reeta climbed up beside Hanna in the front seat of the small wagon. The four brothers were crowded in the back, each one dressed in his Sunday best, with stiff white collars and slicked-back hair. Even Father looked particularly handsome today, though he pulled at his collar and kept readjusting the tie, hoping to gain some breathing space.

The wagon bumped along the dirt road, and others joined them on this fine, crisp Sunday morning, some walking, some riding, and even one or two in small black buggies. The few miles into Puolanka seemed endless to Reeta, wondering when she would catch a glimpse of Thomas. Last week she had hardly noticed him. How could things have changed so quickly?

When they arrived at the church, Father pulled the wagon up alongside several others, and everyone climbed down, scattering here and there in the crowd of churchgoers. Only Matti stayed to tend to the mare, releasing her from the harness and tying her to the nearest tree. Reeta waited by the wagon, searching the crowd.

"Looking for someone?" came a whisper from behind.

She flew around to face the voice. There were the same gray eyes, the same soft brown hair and twitching moustache, but not the same person she wanted to see.

"Well, I guess I can't fool you," Jake said, laughing. "If you're looking for the love-sick, little puppy, he's on the other side of the porch waiting for you."

Reeta didn't bother to reply, only turned and walked toward the porch, hoping the fire in her cheeks would be mistaken for merely the effects of the morning ride in the cool air.

She could still hear Jake's taunting laughter when, coming around the side of the porch, she saw Thomas. He was talking to another young man, but his eyes were scanning the churchgoers until he saw her. For a moment they were the only two people in the whole world, their eyes saying what they could not say aloud.

Thomas excused himself from the conversation, and looking around as casually as he could, walked toward her, stopping only when their coat sleeves brushed together in a whispering sound. "Is it all right, Reeta?" he asked so quietly she could barely hear. "I mean, you still feel the same way?"

Before she could answer, Hanna motioned to her from the doorway, giving her a puzzled look at the same time.

Reeta breathed an answer, her lips barely moving. "I love you, Thomas!" She didn't dare look at his face, but immediately ran up the steps and grabbed Hanna's arm, pulling her into the building. All the way down the aisle to their family pew, the words kept echoing through her mind: *I love you, Thomas. I love you.* She had said it; it was spoken.

Reeta slid along the highly polished dark wood pew, seating herself next to Hanna. The pump organ had begun its wheezing preliminaries, and people were quickly finding their places. During the hymns Reeta hardly knew what she was singing. She could feel his gray eyes watching her, but she dared not look around.

Reverend Heikkila's words cut through her daydreaming. "Brethren, do not say you have the love of Christ in you if you do not obey his commands. There will be many who will say 'Lord, Lord!' but He will say, 'Depart from me, I never knew you.' "

Reeta had always been strong-willed, yet obedient to her parents. Now, however ignorant they were of the fact, this secret was driving a wedge between them. During the closing prayer, she added her own petition for an answer to her dilemma: to keep the secret yet awhile, or to reveal it.

After the service Reeta had no opportunity to speak with Thomas alone. He walked over to their wagon while Matti hitched up the mare. Thomas stood as near to her as possible while he chatted with her brothers.

When Father came, taking the reins from Matti, the boys climbed into the wagon. Thomas offered his hand to help Hanna up, and then did the same for Reeta. As she grabbed for a hold on the wagon, she felt him lifting her effortlessly up to the seat.

"I'll come soon," he whispered, his words as low as the afternoon breeze, passing unnoticed by the others.

Already Father was reining the mare, turning the wagon onto the road home.

Chapter Eight

FACE TO FACE

After almost a week, Thomas still had not shown up at the house or at the meeting place by the rock. Reeta held firmly to her declaration of love, but she was anxious to see him, to confirm the reality of this thing. It had all happened so quickly. Sometimes she was certain she had imagined the whole thing. She longed to talk to him to his face, not in secret whispers hoping no one would hear.

If Hanna suspected anything, she wasn't curious enough to ask questions. Mother and Father seemed too worried about Eli and Andrew to take notice of her either, but Reeta was certain she couldn't stand one more day without talking to someone.

Hanna and Mother washed the supper dishes while the boys heated up the bathhouse. Preparing for their Saturday evening ritual, Reeta gathered up the towels and hard brown soap. With her free hand she grabbed a pail of water before starting across the yard toward the sauna.

Her heart skipped a beat. There was Andrew, standing by the sauna talking with...Thomas. Water sloshed from the pail onto her skirt, soaking her high-topped, black shoes. She paid little notice to the squishing sound her soggy stockings made in her shoes while she continued her unsteady trip across the yard.

When Thomas saw her, he started toward her boldly. The ill-fated pail of water dropped to the ground this time, dumping the rest of its contents in a pool between their feet. For an awkward moment she stared at him, not knowing what to do.

Andrew appeared at her side, grinning broadly. Snatching the towels and soap from her, he retrieved the pail, too. "Here. I'll take these," he offered. "Uh, I think I'd better see to the sauna." Backing through the doorway he nearly tripped over the threshold.

Thomas lost no time reaching out to take her hand. "I tried to get away earlier this week," he apologized, a worried look in his eyes. "Can you forgive me for not coming sooner? Please don't think ill of me."

"Oh, no! Certainly not!" she said, trying not to reveal how much she had worried.

Just then she saw Eli coming around the side of the sauna. He was busy carving on a birch tree branch, all the while whistling a bright little tune. Reeta pulled her hand free, but not before Eli had abruptly ended his tune.

"Well, it's about time you showed up," he greeted Thomas, flexing the branch playfully in his direction. "We have so much planning to do, you know. Or do you have some plans you haven't told me about?"

Andrew had stepped out of the sauna while his brother was talking. He cleared his throat loudly. "Eli, we could use some more of those branches," he suggested, nodding toward the trees behind the bathhouse. "Why don't we get a few?"

"What?" he asked. "Oh, sure! We can always use another good switch for the sauna." The brothers all but ran for the trees, making quite a commotion in the process.

Reeta placed her weight on one foot and then the other, feeling the cold, soggy wool socks clinging to her toes. *What now?* she wondered.

"Reeta," Thomas said, getting directly to the point, "it's not right to keep this secret. I should have talked to your parents before now." He took her hand again, trembling, yet his voice continued bravely, "They may reject my petition, even throw me out of the house, but I must tell them what my intentions are."

She turned pale even thinking about the confrontation. "I know you're right about telling them," she admitted. "We can't be deceitful, but I'm so afraid of what they will say. You don't know how Mother feels about our family being landowners." And the idea of her going to America, too? It was beyond her imagination what they would have to say about that.

"Did you mean it when you said that you loved me?" Thomas asked.

"Yes," she answered, hoping her voice sounded confident enough to convince him.

"Then you must trust me now," he pleaded. "Besides, the time is running short. We leave in only a few months."

Reeta was nearly in tears. She had little faith that their dream would work out when faced with her mother's cold stare.

"Here," Thomas said, leading her to the bathhouse steps. "Sit beside me. I want to tell you something." He sat on the edge of the top step.

She obediently seated herself near him, relieved that he hadn't gone straight to the house.

"You see," he began, "I have been praying for you for a very long time, Reeta. I don't think you even noticed me, but you have been right here in my heart so long." He clasped a hand over his chest.

She listened intently to his confession, amazed that he could tell her such personal things.

"I knew that I didn't have a farm or any earthly possessions to offer," he continued, "and for a couple years I thought it was hopeless. I even prayed that God would send a proper suitor for you, someone who would love you as much as I do. "

Now the tears were flowing; she couldn't stop them. To think that he was so unselfish! Why, her prayers had never been truly for Thomas. She had asked God for what she, herself, had wanted. Surely she had done nothing to deserve this kind of love.

He drew her close, putting his arm around her shoulder until she could gain control of her emotions.

"Don't you see," he said, confidence growing in his voice, "America is our hope. I have a chance now to make something of myself, to have my own land. If God has kept you for me this long, surely He can be trusted to work out this difficulty with your parents."

"Yes," she said softly, wiping her damp cheeks with a sleeve, "I think God might do that for you, but my faith is so small."

"Oh, Reeta," he protested, "you'll see. It will all work out in the Lord's time." Thomas squeezed her in a quick hug. Then, pulling her to her feet, he announced, "Let's go."

Despite his encouragement and fine words, Reeta was certain her knees would give out, turning into mush before they reached the house. Though her body was failing from nervousness, she was surprised to find that, with each step, her heart and mind were more certain than ever. This was right!

When they stepped into the house, no one looked up for a minute. Father was seated by the fireplace, absorbed in the latest newspaper from Oulu. Mother was working in the far corner at the large loom, painstakingly weaving a colorful new rug from leftover scraps of material.

Hanna was the first to notice them. She gave Reeta a surprised look, but said nothing, continuing to put away the clean dishes.

Thomas cleared his throat, venturing, "Good evening, Mr. Wayrynen."

Father looked up, considering him carefully before answering, "Thomas, well what brings you here? The boys are out heating up the sauna."

"Yes, sir," he answered politely, "I wish to talk to you, if I may."

"Here, I'll take your coat," Reeta suggested, glad for the chance to do something. She took off her own coat as well, and hung them both by the door.

Mother left her loom and moved closer, standing beside the hearth. "Have a seat, Thomas," she offered, pointing to a chair across from Father.

Reeta hadn't the slightest notion why Mother was being so polite. Could she have felt sorry for the way she had snubbed Thomas the last time he had appeared at the house? She doubted it.

"Thank you," he said, "but I'd rather stand."

Reeta came to stand beside him, hoping to lend some measure of courage, though she had little to give.

"You folks know," he said, addressing both her parents, "that I am going to America in the spring. My brother Veerus is there already and writes that there is land, much land, waiting to be bought...and cheaply."

"Yes," Father replied, obviously still not happy about his sons. "I can't say that I understand why you would go so far away though."

"If I stay here, sir," he said, "there is little future for me, but there I can have my own farm, build a fine house, and provide a good life...for my wife and family."

Reeta could hardly breathe. The silence pounded in her ears. Father and Mother both registered his meaning at the same moment.

"Yes," Thomas said, confirming their suspicions, "I have asked Reeta if she will wait for me. When I have the farm and house ready, I'll send for her. You've no need to worry. She will be well-provided for. I love her, sir."

Chapter Nine

THINGS FORBIDDEN

Mother lost no time recovering from her surprise. "Thomas Juntunen," she spluttered, "you are terribly presumptuous! Isn't it bad enough that you should talk my sons into this crazy adventure? I had hoped we could convince you to give it up."

So much for Mother's politeness, Reeta thought.

"And now you are not asking us, you are telling us, that you want our daughter to follow after you?" She spoke the words incredulously. "This is absurd!" Placing her clenched fists firmly upon her hips, she stared at him with unwavering eyes of steel.

The forcefulness of Mother's reply startled Reeta. She instinctively reached out, resting a hand on Thomas' arm to let him know she was still there, on his side.

"I assure you," he responded, looking directly at her mother, "I have considered the seriousness of this matter. If you are judging me because I am not a landowner, there is nothing I can do to remedy that. Can any man choose his birth or station in life? But in America everyone has an opportunity to make his own place."

Now, Thomas turned his attention toward Father. "Sir, I love your daughter. If I should fail somehow, if I find I can't get the farm, I would not ask her to be my wife. She deserves no less."

Father stood up, looking into the fire for several moments. He slowly turned his attention first to his still-infuriated wife, and then to the two young people. His face was humorless.

"I don't mean to seem cruel, young man," he began, "but you must respect our ways. We have worked hard to maintain a certain quality of life for our children. Even you, yourself, have said that right now you have nothing to offer our daughter except this dream."

Reeta tensed her body, preparing for the words about to come. This was it. Couldn't Thomas see? How could he be so calm?

"The fact is," Father concluded, "we must forbid you to see Reeta again. There will be no more filling her head with hopeless dreams."

Taking one step, Father moved between the two of them. Reeta couldn't see Thomas' face, only her father's steeled back. Inconsolable tears began trickling down her face, leaving little blotches on her starched white shirtwaist. They were walking toward the door, but she couldn't see through the tears. Muffled voices sounded far away.

It was Thomas speaking. "Have faith, Reeta! They can't take away my dream!"

* * *

She had never cried so much in all her life as she had the past few weeks. This was ridiculous. Or was this the price of love? Love? Why should something so wonderful cause such pain as well?

Arguing with her parents was pointless, defying them unthinkable. The bonds of family could not be broken by romantic feelings, at least not so easily. However, the aching in her heart never seemed to stop, no matter how she tried to distract herself.

Eli and Andrew continued making plans, gathering the things they would need for their journey. Everyone knew it would be a journey of no return.

One Sunday afternoon, Reeta decided to take a walk. She put on her coat, hat, and mittens, not bothering to look at her reflection in the small mirror. She didn't care how she looked. "Mother, I need to get some air. I won't be gone too long."

Mother looked at her curiously, replying, "Why don't you take Aatu with you? He's outside somewhere."

"All right, I'll ask him," she consented, realizing she would never be completely trusted until Thomas was out of the country. No one worked on Sunday, except for the few chores that could not be put off. Milk cows and chickens didn't know or care that it was a day of rest. Having just finished feeding the livestock, Aatu was sorting through a pile of broken handles and scrap wood near the tool shed.

Reeta watched him for a few minutes. He heaved a piece of splintered wood against the shed, and then kicked through the pile of discarded parts, finally throwing another innocent piece angrily in the same direction.

"You're certainly in a fine mood today," she said, wishing she could get rid of some tension as easily.

Aatu stopped and looked her way, his normally pale cheeks blushing with color. "Where are you going?" he asked.

"I wanted to take a walk," she said, "and Mother thinks you should keep an eye on me, I guess."

Aatu nodded. "Perhaps a walk would do me some good, too. Where are you headed? The woods?"

"No," she protested. She couldn't take Aatu to her special place. Memories of Thomas would be too strong. She hadn't been there since... "Why don't we walk toward the village?"

Aatu shrugged his shoulders, joining Reeta as she walked to the main road. She breathed in the crisp air, observing the scenery along the rutted road. Pine trees lined one side of the road and on the other side a gentle hill wandered down to a clear blue lake.

Aatu stopped to gaze at the tranquil lake, calling, "Reeta, do you think there is anything as beautiful as this in America?"

She thought about Thomas. "They say it's much like this," she managed to say with difficulty. "Why? Are you thinking about your brothers?"

"No," was his curt reply. "I don't see why they should be the only ones to go. I mean, I can earn my keep. Eli says I must never mention the idea. Mother and Father need me here."

Reeta looked at him, seeing the longing in his eyes. "I didn't know you felt that way. You've always been so...I mean..."

"So sickly looking? So spoiled?" he shouted angrily. "Can't I have dreams, too?"

She almost began quoting Thomas, but bit her tongue instead, offering advice she only halfheartedly believed. "If that's what you really want, don't ever stop hoping. It may be that we will both see America someday."

"You're a fine one to talk, Reeta," he accused. "Just what hope do you have? Do you think they will change their mind about Thomas? Never!"

"That's not fair!" she cried, starting down the road without him.

"Wait!" Aatu called, trying to catch up with her. "I'm sorry, Reeta. It's just that I don't think there's any use waiting around for a miracle. If you want to join Thomas in America, you'll have to have a little backbone and go without Mother's or Father's blessing. Don't you see?"

Reeta stopped suddenly, looking her younger brother in the eyes. She wanted to scream at him, but she knew that he might be right after all. Without a word, she started walking again, Aatu falling in step beside her.

Around the bend, a small clearing came into view. In the middle sat a house, rather plain in every way except for the flower boxes and fussy curtains at the windows. She hadn't planned it. But why not?

"Let's stop and say hello to the pastor's wife," Reeta suggested.

Aatu raised an eyebrow in surprise, but followed her down the pathway to the house. Before they reached the door, a tall, thin woman appeared, beckoning them with a wave.

"Welcome. Welcome, children," she called.

"Good day to you, Mrs. Heikkila," Reeta greeted her warmly. The woman's sharp features belied her pleasant nature.

"Please, come in," she offered. "I'm so glad for company today. Henri had to go out on a call. And I've all this lovely coffeecake going to waste."

Before long the three of them were seated around a small table in the kitchen, sipping black coffee and devouring the sweet cake. Mrs. Heikkila kept the conversation going in a light, cheerful vein.

"Henry has been so busy since we moved here," she said, rather proudly. "He's not home much during the day, but the people in the congregation are so kind. The Lord certainly blessed us with a lovely home, too. Don't you think so?"

Aatu had been looking at the empty wood box near the stove. "Looks like you could use some more wood," he said. "I'd be glad to get some for you. No trouble at all." He rose before she could protest, going out the door for the woodpile.

"What a sweet young man," Mrs. Heikkila declared. Then she turned her attention toward Reeta. "I don't mean to pry, child, but you look like something is troubling you. May I be of any help?"

That was all the nudging it took. Soon Reeta had spilled out the whole story of the happenings of the past few weeks. Speaking her hopes and fears helped to lessen the burden on her heart. Surely this godly woman would know what she should do.

Mrs. Heikkila patted her hand understandingly. "Child, as I see it, you've done no more and no less than you could up to now. I know it's difficult to wait, but you must, or risk losing God's blessing, too. Thomas is right. If the Lord is in this, then He will change your parents' hearts, but if you take matters in your own hands, well, it would never be as good."

Reeta cringed at her words. Her parents had never, on any occasion that she could recall, changed their minds once they made a firm stand. There was no reason to hope now.   She would live out her life in her parents' home, suffering silently, refusing to marry anyone. If that's what they wanted, that's the way it would be.

Chapter Ten

GOING AWAY

Spring crept in one morning when Reeta wasn't looking. Usually it came with joy and shouts of excitement at the first flowers in the field or tender green buds. This year was different. She had almost dreaded seeing the first signs.

It was the tiny lily-of-the-valley, which heralded the season. Reeta was hanging out the wash on a windy Monday morning when she spotted the little flower in the shade of the clothesline pole. Its small, white, bell-shaped flowers had not yet burst from their green covers, but just the same, its message trumpeted in her ears. Spring! And winter was going away.

Picking up the empty laundry basket, Reeta trudged across to the house. Maybe if she didn't tell, no one would know spring had come. Time could stand still until she was ready to let her brothers go. "Foolish child!" she scolded herself aloud. Eli and Andrew had said they were leaving in the spring. The farm would be so lonely without them; she would be lonely without them.

Then there was Thomas, the name she was forbidden to say. The last six weeks had been so strange. It was as if he had died. Eli and Andrew were going to America with this ghost-of-a-person, but they couldn't speak of him, much less invite him to the house to share in the preparations.

Thomas wasn't the only one who was a ghost. Reeta felt the life had gone out of her the last day she had seen him. Nothing she did now seemed important. No one she saw could cheer her.

Setting the basket on the steps, Reeta stretched and yawned. That was another thing. Sleep. She couldn't sleep, not well that is, but spent hours staring into the darkness and praying for the dawn. Then each new dawn was only to be endured.

"Mother," she heard Eli saying through the door, "Andrew and I have to get the last of our supplies from the store. How about letting Hanna and Reeta come along? They know more about getting a good bargain and all. We really could use their help."

"Yes," joined in Andrew, "if they could come with us, we would feel much better about it. So, what do you say?"

There was a pause. Reeta was sure Mother wouldn't allow her to go to town. Even going to church was forbidden without her Mother's watchful eye.

"Well, I guess it wouldn't do any harm," Mother answered, her voice sounding uncertain.

The brothers tumbled out the front door, grabbing Reeta between them and lifting her into the wagon with a whoop. Hanna followed, reserved and quiet as usual. Reeta had hardly caught her breath before they were on the road to Puolanka.

When they reached the village, it dawned on Reeta that the three young men were not the only ones having purchased passage to America. Several other families were gathered at the store, along with their friends, visiting and talking of plans for the departure, now only days away.

Eli seemed especially anxious. He kept looking about the crowded store, obviously not searching for supplies. Andrew had enlisted Hanna to help him pick out some practical traveling shoes, something Mother couldn't make, while Eli guided Reeta toward the back corner where tools of all kinds lined the wall.

"You want me to help you with this?" Reeta asked, bewildered.

"Well, not exactly," Eli said nervously. "I need your advice about something over here." He led her into a small storage room. One tiny window, high in the back of the stuffy narrow room, was the only source of light, making it difficult to see.

Her eyes were just getting used to the dimness when the door closed behind her. She reached out, groping for the door handle, but it wouldn't budge.

"Reeta!" The whispered word came from behind her.

She turned around slowly, gasping at the sight of a dark, shadowy figure standing a few feet from her. She couldn't move.

"It's me!" a voice whispered. "I had to see you."

"Thomas!" she exclaimed, hardly daring to believe it was him.

"Sh!" he warned, moving toward her.

She would have run to him, but she was stabbed with a pang of uncertainty. Stepping back, she braced herself against the door. "No, no! I can't do this," she cried, shaking her head. "If Father and Mother find out...You don't know how awful it's been. This isn't going to work. Please!"

Lifting her chin gently, he looked into her eyes, now clouded with tears. "My dearest Reeta," he spoke softly, coaxing her, "if I could endure the pain for you, I would gladly take it. A few months ago you were ignorant of my love for you. Now, though it seems impossible, there is a glimmer of hope that someday we will be together. Would you rather I'd never spoken to you?"

"No," she freely admitted. "It's just so hard to believe when nothing seems to be going right."

She didn't resist when he wrapped her gently in his arms. They stood silently several minutes, lost in thought. Then Thomas made a place for them to sit on some sacks of flour, and they talked intently, not wanting to waste a moment.

Reeta suddenly began giggling, trying to muffle the sound with her hand.

"What's so funny?" he asked, puzzled, but glad to see a change from the dark mood.

Reeta caught her breath, telling him how Eli and Andrew had carried her off without an explanation, and then how Eli had tricked her into the storeroom. "He's probably out there right now, standing guard!"

They both were laughing now, enjoying the comedy.

All too soon there was a tap on the door. Eli cracked it open a few inches, saying, "Sorry, but we have to be going in a minute." He grinned sheepishly at them, quietly closing the door again.

Thomas stood up, brushing off the clinging white powder from the flour sacks. He offered his hand to Reeta, helping her get to her feet.

"Listen to me carefully," he said, not letting go of her hand. "As soon as we are settled at the logging camp, I'll send a letter to you letting you know how things look about getting a farm. I don't know how long it will be, but I swear to you that I will send for you."

"But how will I get the letter?" she asked. "My parents surely won't let me have it."

"Perhaps," he said, seeming to have figured it out, "I could put it inside a letter to you from Eli."

"I suppose that might work," she agreed doubtfully.

"But, Reeta," he tried to reassure her, "I'm trusting that the Lord will soften their hearts. I'll keep on praying every day." He hugged her tightly one last time, brushing a kiss across her forehead. "Next time I see you, you will be mine...mine."

The door opened, letting in the light. Thomas squeezed her hand, before disappearing among the supplies. Adjusting her eyes to the light again, Reeta stepped out into the store, trying to act as normal as possible. Eli diverted attention away from her for a few minutes while she composed herself, taking deep breaths.

Hanna was the first to come looking. "What have you two been doing?" She didn't wait for an answer before asking another question, pointing to Reeta's skirt. "What is all that white stuff on your skirt?"

"Oh, it's from the flour sacks," Reeta said, brushing off the white stuff indignantly. "I guess I must have bumped against them in the storeroom."

Andrew crept up quietly between the sisters, whispering, "Hey, isn't that Saara Riihimaki? Over there."

They looked at the people gathered by the front window of the store. A pretty young blonde turned their way, her gaze resting on Eli. She smiled and waved.

Eli smiled eagerly in return. "Just give me a few more minutes," he said, not taking his eyes from Saara. He lost no time working his way around the displays toward the girl.

"The Riihimakis have been making plans, too," Andrew informed his sisters. "It seems they will be heading for Washington only a few months after we are gone. Can you believe that? Nice for Eli, huh?"

Reeta was glad for his good fortune. She had no doubt that Eli would find his happiness then. *Saara is a sweet girl, even if she is quite young,* she thought.

Saara's father slapped Eli on the back, shaking his hand enthusiastically. Smiles from her mother, too. Clearly this was one family who welcomed the attentions of their daughter's suitor. Reeta fought the jealousy rising in her.

On the way home, talk was subdued. Eli was probably dreaming of Saara, Andrew's eyes seemed bright with thoughts of the adventure ahead, Hanna was her inscrutable self, and Reeta tried to relive each moment of her secret encounter.

Chapter Eleven

SEASONS

They had gone one morning before dawn, when the thin sliver of a silver moon lay on the horizon. Father had driven the wagon down the rutted path to the road, eyes straight ahead. Eli and Andrew had waved madly and shouted farewells that echoed across the meadow.

Mother held back her tears until they were out of sight, only then allowing herself to weep openly. Reeta knew her mother's grief was overwhelming, for she believed she would never see her sons again. Weeks passed, Mother refusing to wear anything but black. She mourned their departure as if they had died.

Spring passed without word from the brothers except for a postcard with one brief message scrawled in Andrew's handwriting:

We have arrived. All is well.
Eli and Andrew

Everyone supposed they were either too busy in the logging camps, or too isolated from civilization to get a letter sent out. Reeta prayed it wasn't for lack of good news.

The summer's endless days brought with them no lack of things to do. The girls worked alongside mother, weeding row upon row of precious vegetables, sweet strawberries, and lingonberries. A short growing season only intensified their efforts to make the best of the time. Father, Aatu, and Matti worked long days also--fixing fences, repairing the roof on the house, and caring for the animals. Fields of hay grew tall with their golden offering for the coming winter.

It wasn't until the fall harvesting was nearly complete that Reeta discovered herself the center of attention. Several young men began dropping by the farm, each one having some excuse to see her. Flattering though it was, Reeta protested.

Not that she voiced her disapproval, for she endured their attentions mainly because it seemed to bring some happiness back into her mother's eyes. It was the things she failed to do, the subtle things that Reeta hoped would send a message to these young men without offending them or her parents.

Reeta sat across from a young farmer, sipping coffee and picking at the sweetbread out of politeness. "That's nice," she offered indifferently every once in a while as the young man droned on about his accomplishments. She was amazed at his conceit, his absolute occupation with himself.

"In a few more years," the farmer bragged, "my farm will be producing more milk and beef than any in the area." He looked at Reeta with a "Well-what-do-you-think-of-that?" smile.

She stared back, wondering how Thomas' farm was coming along. "That's nice," she replied, stirring more sugar into her coffee.

Mother buzzed around the table, smiling at the young man. "More coffee?" she asked, pouring it before he could answer. Her eyes were filled with questioning hope when she looked at Reeta.

Reeta sat up straight in the chair, looking down into the dark swirls in her cup. What was it that Mrs. Heikkila, the pastor's wife, had said the last time they had met? Yes, now she remembered.

She had said, "Reeta, have you thought about the possibility that God might not allow you to marry Thomas? If your parents have not changed their minds at all, don't you think you should at least consider their wisdom?"

Consider this? Reeta thought, looking once more into the face of the too-eager young man. He was too tall, too dull. He didn't care about her, only his cows. She would never marry.

Reeta began clearing away the things from the table, hoping the farmer would decide for himself that it was time to leave. "It was nice of you to come by," she said. Why did she keep using that word, nice? Then again, she decided he probably deserved nothing more descriptive.

"Yes," he answered with a smile.

He thinks I'm complimenting him, she thought, astonished.

"I've been meaning to do this for some time," he rationalized, "but the cows, you know."

Right, she thought, *the cows do come first!*

"Now that winter is coming, I'll have more time."

Now that you'll be bored, you mean.

"Could I see you again soon?" he inquired, sure of himself.

"Oh, well," she stalled, hoping, actually praying for a way out of this conversation.

Matti was the answer. He flew into the room, his excitement putting an abrupt end to the young man's question. "Look here!" he exclaimed, waving two envelopes in the air. "Letters from both Eli and Andrew! Here, Reeta, this one from Eli is addressed to *you*."

Reeta's heart flew with anticipation. She stared at the travel-worn envelope in her hands, feeling the weight of it for a few moments.

Mother, however, took the letter from Matti, reaching for the one in Reeta's hand at the same time. When Reeta was reluctant to give it up, Mother said, "We should all be here before we read the letters, don't you think?"

Reeta slowly relinquished hold of the envelope. She wasn't even aware that the young man had excused himself, leaving them to their family business. It was only an hour until Father and Aatu would be in for supper, but to Reeta it seemed they would never come.

The food was on the table even before steps were heard on the porch. Matti ran for the door at the first sound. Though the steaming dishes of potatoes and meat beckoned, Father sat down in his place, pushing his plate aside. He held the letters thoughtfully while the rest of the family took their places.

Carefully opening the first letter with his puukko knife's curved tip, he removed a single neatly-folded sheet, opened it, and began to read:

Dear Family,

We have been working these past months in a logging camp in the hills above Stella on the Columbia River. There are many immigrants here--mostly Finns, Swedes, and Germans. The days have been long--at least ten hours of work. By the time we get our evening meal, we are so tired that we go right to bed. But the wages are good—a dollar a day. We are saving every dollar, along with what we were able to put away after the trip.

Speaking of the trip, the steamship was quite crowded and not very clean, but we were too excited about America to complain much.

Father, you should see the land that we have found for a farm. Thomas...

Father paused, glancing quickly at Reeta. Having already said the name, there was nothing to do but go on.

...Thomas has picked out a place right near ours. The next time we write, we will tell you how it is coming along. We miss you all very much, and send our love.

> *Your sons,*
> *Eli and Andrew*

P.S. The Riihimakis have bought a farm in the same hills. A.J.

The room was silent for a minute, and then Matti said, "Reeta, how about your letter?" Father examined Eli's handwriting on the envelope and passed the letter to Reeta. She dreaded opening the envelope in front of the family. The note from Thomas was inside; she knew it. Holding the letter in her hands, she wondered if she could excuse herself to read it privately.

"Open it, Elsa," her mother prodded.

"Surely there's no secret between the two of you?" Father asked.

"No," Reeta assured him, "certainly not." Reeta slid her finger under the edge of the envelope and gently pulled it open. Breathing deeply, she looked inside and pulled out the letter. As she unfolded the page, she could feel an extra thickness of paper. A smaller envelope fell onto the table. It bore the inscription in neat letters: *Reeta*.

Mother stretched across the table, about to snatch up the envelope, when Father reached out.

"It's addressed to Reeta," he said, restraining her hand. "She must decide what to do with it." There was no doubt that Father meant it.

Picking up the envelope with shaking hands, Reeta looked at her mother. The old bitterness had returned to her eyes. Clutching the small treasure in one hand, Reeta quickly read over the letter from Eli, and then passed it to her father so he could read it to the others.

While he was reading, Reeta got up from the table and walked over to the fireplace. She fingered the envelope uncertainly, not daring to open it, torn between Thomas and obedience to her parents.

Father finished reading Eli's letter. Soon the sound of dinner plates and conversation brought her back from her daydreaming. Mother's shoes click-clicked across the floor.

Reeta threw the small envelope into the fire, watching it being singed brown around the edges. Then it burst into flames. "I'm sorry," Reeta said in confusion, "but I can't eat anything. I need to go for a walk."

Mother nodded knowingly. Grabbing her shawl, Reeta fled out the door.

Chapter Twelve

WINTER HEARTS

She ran until she was out of breath, then only pausing for a minute before hurrying down the path almost overgrown with dense summer bracken. Dark green tendrils pulled at her skirt, staining it with verdant streaks. Low-hanging pine branches caught in her hair; she brushed them aside, uncaring.

Reeta hadn't been to her place on the rock since she had last seen Thomas, but her feet remembered the way. Breaking through the trees, she saw the gray, flat-topped boulder. Running up to it, as to a dear, lost friend, she pressed her cheek against its cool surface and let the tears flow.

When she had nearly exhausted her store of tears, she dried her eyes, rubbing them with her sleeves. Then, placing her feet carefully in the small crevices along the side of the rock, climbed to the top, seating herself near the cliff's edge. Gazing down into the valley, she was comforted knowing it had not changed in her absence. The stream still echoed a welcome from far below, and the vivid purple, yellow, and red of fall seemed more beautiful than ever.

Taking a deep breath of pale blue sky, she released her clenched fist, staring at the crumpled piece of paper that fell into her lap. She hadn't been able to throw it into the fire after the envelope. No matter how disobedient it seemed, she had to read the letter. Hadn't Father said that she should decide what to do with it? She needed to know what Thomas had written.

Lovingly she unfolded the letter, smoothing it out against her leg. But before she began reading, she closed her eyes trying to recall a picture of Thomas, or how he might have looked with pen in hand, writing this letter. The image faded in and out until she gave up the effort. Slowly, savoring each word, she began to read:

> *My Precious Reeta,*
>
> *If you are reading this, my heart is glad, for God has answered my prayers. You are in my heart always.*
>
> *My brother, Veerus, has been true to his word about everything. The pay is good. We have plenty of food, and we share living quarters with six other men in the logging camp. The buildings have only beds, called bunks, and a few pieces of crudely made furniture. We hardly need more since we work long days, only coming here to rest. We are saving a fair sum each week.*
>
> *Eli and Andrew are like family to me. On Sunday afternoons the four of us have been exploring the country for good farmland. I have*

seen acreage on the top of the hills above a place called Catlin. The owner is selling cheaply, having logged off all of the timber he wanted.

Reeta, it is the perfect location for our home. There is a small hollow, with a stream and fruit trees! In my mind I can see exactly the kind of house I will build for us.

Be ready to come when I send for you. Maybe in the spring. Surely your parents will see that I am providing well for your future.

I miss you terribly. When you see the moon come up tonight, know that I am sending my love to you when its gentle rays kiss your face. If you don't think it quite foolish, send your love back again, and each time I see the moon, I will bask in your love, too.

Good-night, my dearest Reeta.

Thomas

I can't believe he could write like that, and to me, she thought in wonder. *Will this gentle man never fail to surprise me?* She searched the horizon, wishing the night messenger would be there already.

When at last Reeta was ready to go home, she folded the letter, putting it safely in her apron pocket. Walking back to the house, she began thinking of ways to persuade her parents about Thomas. But each time she thought of a good argument, it soon sounded unconvincing.

By the time she reached the door she knew once again that any persuasion would have to come from God working in their hearts. Saying a prayer, she put her hand to the latch.

Reeta hung her shawl by the door, studying herself in the small mirror. She picked out some twigs that had clung stubbornly to her hair. Smoothing back the straight brown locks, she caught them neatly into the bun at the nape of her neck. *There must be a way*, she lectured herself.

Turning around, she saw Father watching her intently. Mother was cleaning up the dishes, a sullen look on her face. She wouldn't look at Reeta.

"Come here," Father called, motioning to the place across from him at the table. "I want to talk to you."

She sat down expecting to hear another lecture on her responsibilities in life. But Father folded his callused hands together on the table, bringing his head down low to look her directly in the eyes.

His white beard softly dusted the embroidered tablecloth as he spoke, "I know you think we have been hard on you, child."

She started to protest, but remained silent. Not wanting to meet her father's eyes, she focused on the wall behind him.

"Anything we've done is for your good." He faltered, clasping and unclasping his hands. He looked at Mother, then back to Reeta. "Your mother has not changed her mind about Thomas. He is not of the proper class for you, and I can't argue with her reasons. But I do know one thing..."

Reeta looked at him again hopefully.

"...and that is, that he is a fighter. I don't think he will give up until you are his wife. Also, Eli and Andrew think highly of him. They told me before they left. We had quite a long talk on the way to Oulu."

It had never occurred to Reeta that her brothers would dare to take her side openly or argue for Thomas.

"What I am trying to say is that if you have your heart set on this thing, I will not stand in your way."

She looked at her father dumbfounded.

"It breaks my   heart to think of you leaving us, too," Father said, tears forming in his eyes, "but I have seen that your heart is no longer with us. Keeping you here will only turn us against each other." He reached out, patting her hand.

It was not like her father to talk so. She knew it must be very difficult for him. God had heard their prayers.

"Father..." she could only manage to say.

Mother made a sound in her throat and stomped out of the room.

"Try to understand your mother," he pleaded. "She doesn't want to lose you. It makes it even harder knowing you will be so far away. Give her time."

"I don't think I could go," Reeta said, almost choking on the words, "unless Mother approves. I don't want to hurt her."

"Be patient," he advised. "It may work itself out yet."

* * *

Fall passed into winter, silent snow blanketing the meadow. Little white bumps protruded where the sauna and outbuildings stood, larger ones identifying the barn and house. The rail fences marking the borders of the pasture lay like white lace zigzagging across the horizon.

No one ventured out much except from necessity to feed the animals or gather in a new supply of wood. The sauna was, of course, a necessity also. After Aatu and Matti had started the fire to heat up the bathhouse, they waited until the smoke and gas had vanished.

The women were first to enjoy the ritual. Pouring some of the heated water over the hot rocks with a long-handled, wooden ladle, Reeta took a deep breath as billows of steam filled the room. Mother and Hanna sat on the high benches switching themselves now and then with the small birch branches, which increased blood circulation. When the bathers had thoroughly perspired, they washed, rinsed with cold water, and dressed. Feeling clean inside and out, Reeta followed Mother's tracks in the snow back to the house.

The men were not so sedate about their turn at the sauna. Reeta could hear the boys' laughter as they ran across the yard. When they had finished steaming and washing, she could hear their whooping yells echoing across the meadow as they rolled in the snow before dressing.

Father and the boys spent long evenings making new tool handles or carving intricate design work with their sharp-bladed puukkos. No Finn would be without his puukko knife. With it he could do most any job, from building a house to slicing his bread.

Mother shared the loom with her daughters, producing sturdy plain material for clothing as well as colorfully striped wool rugs. They embroidered delicate floral designs on aprons, blouses, and tablecloths.

With the winter had come a sense of timelessness, even Reeta feeling a suspension from life and problems. The sun stayed up for only six hours, but the long nights were illuminated by the Northern Lights. She often sat by the small-paned window watching the colors play across the sky or gazing at her messenger moon.

There was ample time also for reflection and reading. Several more letters had come from America, telling of their progress and plans. Reeta had written to Thomas about Father's somewhat strained consent and Mother's unwavering opposition. "You must choose," she read Thomas' words. "Whatever you decide, be certain you can do it with your whole heart. A wrong choice now will only lead to bitterness in the days ahead."

She knew what she must do.

Chapter Thirteen

UNEXPECTED PASSENGER

The snow was melting, dropping in great plops on the forest floor. Spring was trying to awaken the dream-like winter when the letter arrived. Reeta had expected it, but perhaps not so soon. It had been a little more than a year since Thomas and her brothers had left for America.

When she first felt the letter, she knew it was time. Her fingers trembled as she opened the envelope and pulled out two tickets, one bearing the name of the steamship company and the other, the transcontinental railroad.

"Come before September," Thomas wrote. "There are several departure dates listed. Be sure to confirm when you will be coming. I'm only sorry that I couldn't afford better than steerage. Can you believe it? Our dream will soon be real!"

Looking at the tickets, Reeta knew it was real, but it frightened her, too. She kept trying to remember how Thomas looked and how it felt to have his arms around her.

It was no use. The image had faded; the feelings were a memory. Now all she could picture was her mother's hurt look when she told her what she had decided.

She was going to America. All the doubts she had ever entertained came to the surface as she held the tickets in her hands. Her decision to go was not based on emotion, but a commitment, a promise she had made to Thomas. She had made her choice with her whole heart, and now there was no turning back.

"Well, what have we here?" Father asked, sitting down beside her at the table.

She handed the tickets to him. "I guess it's just a matter of deciding which passage date."

"You know I still don't like the idea of your going all that way by yourself," he worried aloud.

Aatu was standing behind them. "Father, I could go with her." They both turned at the same time, looking into the hopeful eyes of her younger brother. Why hadn't she thought of it before now? The pieces fit. He had been dropping hints for weeks, making his suggestions jokingly. She had been too absorbed with her own plans, but now she saw how serious he was.

"You?" Father questioned, a surprised look on his face.

"Me," Aatu affirmed. "I haven't spoken seriously of this before, because..."

"Because it's crazy," Father finished the sentence.

"No, listen to me," he begged. "Even before Eli and Andrew left, I wanted to go and see what America is like. It's been consuming me."

"Absolutely not," Father bellowed, slapping his hand roughly on the table. "I'll not have all my children eaten up by that great cannibal nation."

Reeta touched his hand gently. "But, Father, don't you see? Aatu could come with me and then if it didn't work out," she added, looking hopefully at Aatu, "he could earn enough money and return the next year."

Father had protested. Mother had nearly fainted at the thought, still picturing him as her sickly child. But Aatu had argued his case well; he was going.

From that morning on, there was so much to be done in preparation that Reeta had little time to think. The old trunk with leather straps had to be packed with care, deciding what was essential and what would have to be left behind.

Hanna insisted on some delicately embroidered sheets that were to have been for her own wedding. Matti included a gift for Thomas--a new puukko, its sharp blade sheathed and its handle ornately carved by his own hand. Father added a leather-bound volume--a Bible that had been given to him by his father. Poor Mother would have no part in sending her daughter away. But the morning she was to leave, Reeta found a new, brightly-colored rug wedged into a corner of her trunk.

"Reeta, you still can end this foolishness," Mother had offered. "Don't you love me at all?" The pleading look in her eyes was piteous to behold.

"Mother," she had answered, more firmness in her voice than she thought she could manage, "if I stay, I will only grow into a bitter old woman. Neither of us would be happy. I do love you, but I must go. "

She had gone; no hugs or farewells from her mother, only icy coolness. Everyone else had come to see them off, Father driving the wagon to the port at Oulu, and Hanna and Matti going along for the ride.

In all her life Reeta had never been to a city as large as Oulu, called "The White Town of the North." Riding through the city, she stared at the crowds, large buildings, and narrow streets all squeezed together. Every few minutes she grabbed for Hanna or Aatu, begging them to look at some new sight.

The port was even more crowded than the city itself. People were shoving and pushing or gawking about, inadvertently blocking traffic. How could they possibly know where to go? Father shouted at a group of men near the wagon. They pointed to a small ship docked nearby, where passengers were already boarding for the first leg of their journey. The wagon came to a stop in what seemed to be a waiting area. Father climbed down, motioning to the girls to follow while Matti saw that the horse was tied securely.

"Remember to keep your tickets with you at all times," Father warned. "If anyone questions you, just show them the tickets."

"Yes," Reeta answered, feeling for them in her pocket. "Don't worry." She wished she were as confident as she sounded.

"I'll take care of her," Aatu reassured him. He was staring at the crowd, a faraway gleam in his eyes.

"You write to us as soon as you arrive," Hanna ordered, her voice nearly cracking. She gave Reeta and Aatu each an awkward hug.

Matti hugged his brother quickly and gave Reeta a peck on the cheek. "Better watch out for thieves," he suggested. "You ought to keep your money hidden in your clothes. Some people will stoop to anything."

Father glanced at the line of people, and then looked at Reeta and Aatu. "God bless you, my children," he said, choking back the tears. "God protect you and keep you!" Having uttered the benediction, he hugged each of them.

Reeta couldn't help crying. She put her hand over her mouth to stifle the sobs. "I love you, Father!" she managed to say.

"We'd better get these things to the ship," Matti interrupted, having hoisted the trunk onto his back.

Father and Aatu quickly followed, taking the larger bags, while the girls grabbed some smaller satchels. Coming to the line, they huddled together waiting their turn to board.

The ticket agent briskly examined their tickets, motioning up the ramp, "Passengers only."

Aatu took the trunk from Matti, grabbing a couple bags with his free hand. Somehow Reeta managed the other bags. They crossed the ramp to the deck, finding a place to set down their load by the rail. The ship was nearly ready to leave. Reeta searched the crowd on the dock, locating the three familiar faces. They were waving frantically.

All too soon, the passengers felt the jerk of the ship moving slowly away from the dock. Reeta and Aatu waved until the people were no longer distinguishable. Her tears quickly dried as the wind off the water blew across her face.

"Attention! Attention!" a voice boomed across the deck. "All passengers will please keep their baggage with them. Find a place on the forward deck and remain there until you are assigned accommodations. Our next stop is Stockholm. We will arrive at our port of embarkation in England within the week."

The passengers were directed toward the crowded deck where they piled their trunks and bags in heaps, guarding them or using them for seats. Aatu led the way to a vacant spot by the rail, a lone man seated there with his back toward them.

"Pardon me," he said, tapping the gentleman on the shoulder, "but is this space taken?"

There was something familiar about the man, Reeta thought. The cut of the shoulders underneath the dark coat, the sandy brown hair... She dropped her bags, startled by the face of the young man who stood to greet them.

"Well, who would believe this?" he asked, laughing heartily at her surprise. "This space is free. Do join me."

Aatu was the first to speak. "Jake! Whatever are you doing here?"

"The same thing you are, I suppose," he responded, still eyeing Reeta and enjoying her discomfort.

"But I thought you were...I mean I thought you had no interest in America," Reeta said, stumbling over the words. She still couldn't believe Thomas' twin brother could be on the same ship. Something about it didn't seem right.

"Oh, well, a person can change his mind can't he?" he asked innocently. "Anyway, all the good prospects for marriage seem to have disappeared from the village." He winked at Reeta jokingly.

Reeta had always thought that Jake was crude. She didn't laugh at his suggestive remark, but frowned coolly, scooting her bags as far away from him as she could. Aatu set his baggage down between them offering himself as a diversion for Jake. Why did he have to show up here? Something about him made Reeta uneasy. Whether he intends to or not, Jake would bring them trouble. She knew it.

Chapter Fourteen

THE FIRST LEG

"May I see your tickets, please?" a steward inquired, having worked his way down the row of passengers to Jake.

"Right here," he responded, handing over the ticket he had been clasping tightly in his hand.

"Second cabin," the steward said, checking Jake's name against his list. "Juntunen. You may follow the people in that line." He indicated a line moving slowly to his right.

Jake picked up his baggage. "See you later, I guess," he said, smiling too big.

Reeta and Aatu held out their tickets next. She wondered how Jake had come up with the money to go second cabin. Wants to impress the ladies or find a rich wife, no doubt.

"Steerage. Wayrynen." the steward hesitated, looking up and down a long list. "Yes, here we are. Please go that way." He pointed toward a much longer line forming on the opposite side of the deck.

They gathered their baggage once more, making their way to the steerage passenger line. A few feet at a time, they worked their way down to the lower deck, ending up at last in a large sleeping room. Berths had been placed side by side, allowing only enough space between the rows to walk single file.

"Men, over here," another steward ordered. "Women, that way please." There was only a flimsy partition dividing the two compartments.

Reeta shuffled down the aisle, depositing her bags on the first lower berth she could find.

"See here, young lady," a matronly woman ordered. "You must go down to the end. You're blocking the aisle."

"Sorry," Reeta excused herself, grabbing her bags again. She obediently carted them as far as she could, finally dropping them in the aisle by an empty berth. "You want the bottom one?" she asked, hoping for permission to take it.

"Actually, I prefer the top," the young woman who had been there first, responded. "That way people aren't stepping on your bed trying to climb up. But I'll be as careful as I can. Thanks." She climbed up to her berth, turning around in it like a cat seeking a soft place to lie down.

Reeta lifted her bags out of the aisle, pushing them to the foot of her berth.

"Say, there," the voice came from above her again, "what's your name? Mine is Sonja Hayrynen, from Vaasa."

Reeta stood up to introduce herself, but before she could say a thing the flaxen-haired girl interrupted.

"Could you hand me my bags, there?" she asked, waving her hand impatiently over the side of the berth.

Reeta lifted the bags up to her one at a time, and then said, "My name is Reeta Wayrynen, from Puolanka."

"Yes?" she said, leaning over the edge of the berth, a bright smile creasing the corners of her mouth. "Why that makes us neighbors almost! And what is your destination?"

"America," she answered simply.

"Of course, but where?"

"Oh, yes...Astoria, Oregon," she pronounced the strange sounding words.

Sonja let out a low whistle. "Dearie me! That's a long way." She wiggled around again, this time hanging her stocking feet over the side.

"I now, my father and I, that is, we're headed for New York. Tired of living in a little speck of a village. You are traveling with someone?"

"My brother," Reeta said, suddenly remembering him. "Must we stay here, in this compartment?"

"Well," Sonja said, looking down the aisle, "I imagine they would get into a real temper if we were to go wandering around before everyone is assigned a compartment."

Reeta looked at the matron giving orders to the latest arrivals. She agreed, deciding to try out the berth instead. She lay down thinking over the events of the day. After punching at the lumpy mattress a time or two, she fell asleep.

Sonja was sitting on the edge of her berth when she woke up. "Going to come have a little supper with us?" Sonja asked. She had changed into fresh clothes and braided her golden hair into a single braid, falling down her back.

Reeta rubbed her eyes wondering how long she had been asleep. Having slept with her coat on, she sat up feeling crumpled and out of sorts. Only the rumbling in her stomach compelled her to move. She hadn't eaten anything since early that morning. "I guess I am hungry," she answered, trying to climb out of the berth and arrange her clothing back into some kind of order. "Just give me a minute."

"Sure," Sonja complied, jumping up to grab a shawl from the top berth.

Reeta removed her coat, first transferring the tickets and important papers to her skirt pocket. Then, after combing her hair back into reasonable neatness, she followed Sonja to a line forming at the end of the compartment. They worked their way down a long narrow passageway and into another large compartment, where the smell of food greeted them. Reeta looked around the room for Aatu as they proceeded through the line.

A gruff-looking steward shoved a tin dish, cup and spoon, into her hands. "These are your responsibility," he warned, as though he were a reluctant benefactor of some great treasure. "When you have finished eating, you may wash them over there." He pointed toward a faucet and sink behind the table.

Food had been brought into the dining room in huge galvanized tin cans. A cook's helper ladled out a portion of the meat and vegetables onto her dish, slopping some over on the table. He said something in a foreign tongue. His voice sounded rude to Reeta, almost as if he were scolding her for his carelessness.

"See that you keep a civil tongue, thank you," Sonja spoke up, glaring at the man.

He obviously didn't understand her words, but caught her meaning nonetheless. His only answer was to slop a ladle of food onto Sonja's plate also. A hard biscuit and a cup of tea or milk completed the meal. Sonja led the way to a vacant table, motioning for Reeta to sit across from her.

Reeta looked at the food in front of her, and then looked around to see if anyone were watching. Sonja began wolfing down her food hungrily, not paying attention to her, so Reeta bowed her head, folded her hands in her lap, and said a brief prayer of thanks. When she looked up, Sonja grinned.

"I'm glad to see someone in this world has not forgotten her manners," she said, reaching for the biscuit. "My goodness! This thing feels hard as a rock. "

"My wish would be for some nice, dark coffee," Reeta said, staring at the cup of milk. "It wouldn't be so bad then, maybe." She ate the food not from eagerness, but knowing she would need the strength it gave.

"There you are!" a familiar voice interrupted. "Do you have room for me?"

"Aatu!" Reeta said. "Here, I can make room. I'll move down a little."

"This must be your brother?" Sonja asked, giving him a thorough inspection.

"Yes, excuse me," Reeta apologized putting her hand on his arm. "Sonja, this is my brother, Aatu. Aatu, Sonja."

"Happy to meet you," she said, still staring. "Ah, but it's easy to tell the two of you are related…the same eyes, same nose, and same high forehead."

It had never occurred to Reeta that they looked the least bit alike. She eyed him now in a new light. It must be that being too close blinded you to things strangers could easily see.

After washing their plates and utensils in the sink with lukewarm water, they went back to the sleeping compartments to put them away.

"Remind me to bring along soap and a towel tomorrow," Reeta said in disgust. "Imagine trying to wash greasy plates with barely warm water?"

"I don't mean to pry," Sonja said, changing the subject, "but is your brother feeling well? I mean he looks so pale."

Reeta would have taken offense had she not detected the concern in Sonja's voice. "Oh, that's just him, I guess," she replied. "He's been that way since he was terribly sick as a child. It's nothing. "

"Come along then," Sonja urged, not pursuing the point further. "Let's find out what's going on up on the deck. I need to talk to my father. See you there." She grabbed her coat, not waiting for a reply.

Reeta left her berth only after doing her best to wipe out the plate with a small towel. She wondered what it would look like after a week of such ill treatment.

Aatu met her on the deck. He was beside himself with excitement about their first day at sea, offering detailed explanations about various aspects of the ship. Finally finding a spot near the rail, Reeta stood close to her brother, breathing in the fresh evening air. She stared into the inky black waters of the Gulf of Bothnia, knowing this night was the first of many. Life could never be the same as it had been even yesterday. She didn't feel much like a brave adventurer.

"Lord, forgive me for complaining," she prayed. "These few discomforts are not so great. Bless my family tonight...and bless Thomas." She silently observed the smiling new moon.

During the next few days, the little ship took on passengers in Stockholm and Copenhagen. Every berth was full in the ladies' compartment. Aatu said some men were even sleeping on the floor on his side. The mix of languages and constant activity helped pass the time quickly. Everyone knew it was only a short time longer till they could leave the ship for a stopover in England.

"Reeta! Reeta!" Sonja called down the narrow aisle. She wiggled her way around women and children until she found Reeta carefully repacking her bags. "Leave that for now. Come! You must see it. England is coming into view."

Sonja grabbed her arm, pulling her through the crowded aisle and up the stairs to the deck. There it was indeed—a large port, ornate buildings, warehouses, and ships of all sizes. The first leg of the trip was nearly over. Sonja hugged Reeta in her excitement.

Glancing at the upper deck just then, Reeta saw a wide grin and frantically waving arm. Jake was making a spectacle of himself. She turned back to the rail, but not before she heard her name echoing across the deck.

Chapter Fifteen

INTERLUDE

Passengers from the upper deck left the ship first, moving in a great swarm across the narrow ramp and along the wharf to a large open lot. Reeta hoped Jake would be lost in the crowd being taken on ahead to the hotel.

Sonja and her father, a tall quiet man in his late forties, more or less adopted Reeta and Aatu, making certain they weren't lost in the press of steerage passengers now ready to disembark the small ship. Waiting in line, Sonja tried once again.

"Come now, Reeta," she begged, talking as quietly as she could. "Who was that young man calling to you across the deck? You must know him if he called your name. Please tell me; I'm dying to know. "

Reeta checked to see if anyone was listening. Aatu and Mr. Hayrynen were deep in conversation about cows, or something. She looked directly into Sonja's bright, curious eyes. "Very well," she conceded, "but you mustn't say a word to anyone. His name is Jake Juntunen, and he is the twin brother of Thomas, the man I am going to marry in America."

Sonja's eyes opened wide in excitement. This must have been the best bit of gossip she had heard in years. "But if that's true," she whispered, "how could you dare to snub him like that?"

"I don't like Jake; I don't trust him." Reeta admitted, though it was hard to point to the exact source of her fears. She supposed it could be simply his irritating way of teasing, but there was something else, something indefinable about Jake that grated against her spirit.

"He seemed to be interested in you."

"Nonsense!"

"No, really," Sonja insisted. "Maybe he's following you because...because he's madly in love with you, too." Sonja seemed to be thoroughly enjoying her fantastic imagination.

"Stop that this minute," Reeta fumed. "Not another word."

The conversation came to an end when the crowd began moving toward the ramp. The passengers quickly picked up their baggage, trying not to drop anything as the line pressed closer together.

By the time they had crossed the gangplank and felt their feet on solid ground, several lorries had pulled up on the wharf. The first passengers off the ship were now scrambling to throw their baggage on the back of one of the wagons, then climbing on, too, before the wagons were full.

Out of the corner of her eye, Reeta could see Jake standing in the back of a lorry. Even here he had the air of being lord and master of the situation, his arms folded across his chest while he surveyed the commotion. She ducked behind Sonja, lest he catch sight of her. Maybe she could avoid him at least a bit longer.

Soon it was their turn. Aatu heaved the trunk and bags up first, before leaping up neatly himself, and then offering his hand to Reeta. In a few minutes she and Sonja were settled, safely perched atop a trunk, as the lorry slowly pulled away from the wharf heading into the city.

As they moved along the narrow cobblestone streets, children ran beside the lorry pointing at them and shouting playfully. It was only a brief time before they pulled up in front of a hotel owned by the steamship company. Reeta was glad. She didn't enjoy being considered a novelty to stare at, even if they were just children.

The passengers evacuated the lorries hastily, anxious to see some better accommodations.

"You know what I want first?" Reeta asked, directing her question to Sonja.

"What?" she responded, staring about the spacious hotel lobby.

"A bath!" Reeta exclaimed. "I think nothing else would matter if I could just be clean again."

"Yes," Sonja agreed, "and maybe we can wash our clothes, too.

A matron stepped from behind the desk, eyeing them politely. She wore the uniform of the steamship company: a neatly ironed shirtwaist with the company's name stitched across the pocket and a dark skirt.

"Ladies," she addressed them with a lift of an eyebrow, perhaps to show her importance, "please bring your things and follow me."

Reeta and Sonja barely had time to pick up their bags before the matron was off, marching down a long hallway and up several flights of stairs. Behind her, Reeta could hear others following, bumping their heavy bags against the wooden steps.

They stopped in the doorway of one large room. "The first ten of you will stay here," she stated simply, then counted them off like so many sheep.

Reeta stepped into the room first, hardly believing such luxury. Each bed was neatly made with sheets, blankets, and pillows. The floors were cleaned to a fine polish. Electric lights hung from the ceiling, and steam heat warmed the room with a cozy hissing sound.

Before they had even deposited their baggage near a bed, the matron was back, ready to give a tour of some kind. The women left their things, following her about halfway down the hall.

She opened a large door, leading them into a high-ceilinged room that echoed with every footstep. The walls were of marble and tile, gleaming under the electric lights. Along one wall was a row of small sinks for washing, a mirror fastened squarely above each. "You will find soap and towels of your own here on this shelf," she instructed, speaking clearly, but with a heavy British accent, "and there are bathing facilities through that door." She pointed beyond the sinks. "Here are the water closets," she said, directing their attention to a long row of doors on the other side of the room. Opening one door, she grabbed the chain hanging by the wall, pulling it until water whooshed around inside the gleaming white bowl. "See that you take care to keep this place as neat as you found it," she warned. "Any questions?"

If they had any, no one dared to ask. Reeta looked at Sonja, unable to imagine anyone having one of those things in the house. Both of them giggled under their breath.

"After you freshen up, ladies," the matron continued, "there will be food in the dining room at the bottom of the stairs. Please don't be too long." She disappeared quietly down the hallway.

The women stood there for a minute, not knowing what to do. Then Sonja grabbed a towel and soap, saying, "I'm going to have a bath first."

Immediately the place was alive with activity. Reeta was certain nothing had ever felt as grand in all her life as that steaming bathtub. She probably would have elected to stay there much longer had not Sonja insisted that the food was likely much better than aboard the ship, too.

Reeta was still braiding her damp hair when Sonja could stand it no longer. "If you don't mind, I'll run ahead to inspect the dining room," she offered.

"That's fine," Reeta assured her. "I won't be much longer. Besides, I'm getting quite hungry myself. Maybe you could find your father and Aatu. Save me a place."

"Right," Sonja called, already on her way out the door.

Reeta felt around in one of her bags for the little wooden box. She was sure she had packed it. Yes, there it was. A tiny, delicately carved lid came off revealing a gold-framed cameo. Father had insisted on the extravagant present on her last birthday. She pinned the brooch carefully at the neck of her dark Sunday dress. Why not dress up a little? She touched the delicately carved brooch lovingly before slipping the small box back into her bag.

On the main floor, there were two dining rooms directly across from each other. When Reeta arrived in the hallway, she stood near the doorway trying to find Sonja or Aatu.

"We must stop meeting like this," announced a voice at her elbow.

She didn't have to look at him. Jake would be wearing that conceited smile of his, and she was not going to give him the satisfaction of any reaction on her part.

"Have you seen Aatu?" she inquired coolly, still looking at the rows of diners enjoying their meal.

"Actually, that's why I'm here," he said. "Right this way, please." He indicated the dining room across the hall.

There was nothing to do but follow as he led the way down an aisle to a large table. Mr. Hayrynen, Sonja, and Aatu were already seated. Jake pulled out the reserved chair beside his own, and Reeta sat down. Sonja gave Reeta a roll of the eyes when Jake wasn't looking. Reeta wanted to kick her under the table, but couldn't reach her.

Despite Jake, Reeta thoroughly enjoyed the meal. The gleaming white china was such as she had never seen. "Someday I'll have a set of dishes like this," she said to Sonja.

Sonja seemed more interested in what was on the china...chicken baked in an exotic sauce, crisp greens, and a lovely baked potato. "This is wonderful," she agreed.

Afterwards, Sonja tried the English tea, but Reeta couldn't abide the weak stuff. "It still looks like dirty water to me," she whispered to Sonja.

Sonja made a face across the table, and they both enjoyed a good laugh.

Jake spoke to Reeta, keeping his voice low enough for only her to hear. "It's good to see you enjoying yourself."

She thought there was a note of sincerity in his voice.

"I wanted to apologize, too," he continued. "No matter what you think, I didn't mean to barge into your life. My being here is strictly coincidental. I'm hoping that we can be friends."

She smiled politely, not saying anything, only wondering once again why she couldn't trust him.

That night, drinking in the luxury of her surroundings, Reeta closed her eyes. She wiggled her toes between the clean white sheets, pressing her cheek against the fluffy down pillow. Before falling asleep, she tried to picture Thomas. Every time she thought she had the image clearly in mind, his eyes caught a glimmer of light, and it wasn't Thomas. It was Jake.

Chapter Sixteen

STEERAGE

Reeta stared at the immense ocean liner docked in front them. No pictures or descriptions had quite prepared her the sight of its large, gray side looming above their heads. Upper decks and smokestacks reached impressively into the sky. This monster of a ship would be their home for the next sixteen days.

"Say, you sailing aboard the ship today?" a weary voice inquired. A young matron bundled in several layers of clothing clutched the jackets of two squirming children.

"Yes," Reeta answered, shifting her gaze from the steamship.

"We've been waiting here for three days already," she said, yanking one curious child nearly off his feet. "Seems we were misinformed about the sailing date. Certainly hope they have things in order now." The woman disappeared into the crowd, the two children each trying to pull her in the opposite direction.

"Reeta," Aatu shouted, "look over there!"

"What?" she asked, looking where he pointed.

"The gangplank where we board. They're putting it in place."

In a matter of moments, a sea of people began moving toward the long ramp with wooden rails that led into the belly of the ship.

"Wait for me!" Sonja called, catching up with Reeta. "I don't want to lose you in this crowd."

As they moved toward the ship, Reeta could see another ramp above them leading to the upper decks. Jake would be there somewhere. Wouldn't Mother have been upset about this turn of events? Imagine a poor tenant farmer going second-cabin, and a landowner's daughter in steerage. Mother. Reeta wished their farewell had been on better terms, but now was no time to think of that.

The heavy wooden ramp moaned under the press of the crowd. Reeta thought her arms would surely fall off before she reached a place to rest. Aatu didn't complain, but balanced the heavy trunk on his back with one hand, carrying several smaller bags with the other.

This time, to Reeta's surprise, the steward didn't separate the men and women passengers. All of them were directed to a single enormous room, much larger than they had shared in the previous ship. The berths were made of iron, built in two tiers, having only a low partition between each berth. The lack of privacy was an unexpected blow to many, or so it seemed. Men, women, and children stood in the aisles staring about the huge room. Reeta wondered if there was some mistake.

Aatu was the first to move. "Listen," he whispered huskily. "Reeta, listen to me."

She looked at him helplessly, still not able to believe such treatment.

"Follow me," he ordered, heading quickly down one long aisle, banging the trunk against the iron berths in his haste.

Not knowing what else to do, Reeta, Sonja, and her father all followed him. They came to the end of an aisle where a few of the berths were more private, being alongside the cold gray wall.

"Here, you two take these bottom berths facing each other," Aatu directed Sonja and Reeta. Then looking at Sonja's father, he said, "We'll take the top ones."

Mr. Hayrynen nodded. Before moving any farther, he stared around the room again, seemingly to make some quick calculations. "My Lord," he said, whistling softly, "there must be three hundred, maybe four hundred berths in this place."

"All the more reason to make our claim on this corner," Aatu said, beginning to put some of the smaller bags into the skimpy cupboard and baggage space allotted each berth.

Reeta could have cried, indeed she began busily setting things in order in hopes that the tears would not start. At the hotel there hadn't been time to wait for her clothes to dry thoroughly, so she removed the damp items from a large satchel, hanging them over the one towel rack available. She carefully hid her undergarments beneath a damp skirt and shirtwaist.

Sonja had begun arranging her berth, not speaking for a long time. Finally she sat on the edge of the iron bed, tears running down her cheeks.

"I just can't believe this," she said, frustration lacing each word. "Look at this!" She held up several pieces of straw that had come from the mattress covered by a coarse white canvas.

Reeta was one step ahead of her. "Oh, but Sonja," she said in mock excitement, "did you see the lovely soft pillows we have here?" She held up half of a life preserver that had been shoved under the mattress at the head of her berth.

Soon the men joined in, laughing with them at their mutual predicament. It was Mr. Hayrynen's turn. "For once I wish that God had made me just a little shorter. What do you think?" He held up the lightweight, gray blanket, the only covering issued to each berth. It fell from his chin right down to about the middle of his knees.

One look at his sheepish grin and the short blanket sent the girls into another fit of laughter. When she caught her breath, Reeta pulled at Aatu's sleeve. He knelt down in the aisle close to her berth.

"Yes?" he inquired, still smiling from the joke.

"Thanks," she said, touching his broad shoulder. She pulled at a stray thread hanging from the seam of his jacket.

"For what?"

"For taking care of me…for coming along," she said. "I don't know what I would have done without you." She gave him a quick hug.

"Now don't start getting all sentimental on me," he fussed, sitting back on his heels. He was about to say something else, but hesitated.

"What?" she asked curiously.

"Oh, nothing," he said, wrinkling his forehead into little lines. "Some other time."

The noise from the passengers boarding had grown into quite a terrible din, until a shrill whistle silenced the crowd. Reeta stood up trying to see the man yelling instructions, but it was no use. Listening carefully, an ear tilted in the direction of the voice, she discovered he wasn't speaking Finnish...probably English. The words ended. After a pause the man began again, this time in Swedish, then Norwegian or Danish, and finally in Finnish.

"Please find a berth and stay there until you are given further instructions," boomed the voice from the middle of the room. "We will be sailing within the hour."

Soon the hum of conversation began again, the noise like waves of the ocean, moving in and out with intensity. Reeta lay back in her berth trying to stretch out. Her feet bumped into something at the end of the bed. Reaching under the cover, she pulled out what appeared to be a workingman's lunch pail with a fork, spoon, and cup inside.

"Don't forget your soap and towel," she reminded Sonja, waving the pail. No doubt they would be required to clean their own eating utensils here also.

Sonja searched her berth, finding an identical tin pail also. Holding it up to the light, she whispered excitedly, "Someday I will have a set of dishes as lovely as these!"

Reeta smiled at her, rolling her eyes Sonja-fashion. If they could only keep a sense of humor about their difficulties, it might not be so bad. One could hope.

The huge ship lurched a little to the left, the compartment growing quiet as the passengers listened, awaiting confirmation that they were finally underway. Several minutes later a steward announced that the passengers were now free to leave their berths.

Aatu lost no time jumping down from the top berth. "Come along, folks," he said cheerily. "Let's see what's going on in the world."

The three followed as he forged a path down the narrow aisle. From the large sleeping room, they entered a dimly lit hallway, passing several unidentified doors before Aatu signaled to them from up ahead.

"You'll never believe this," he said, beckoning her with his hand. A look through another doorway revealed a compartment as large as the one they had come from, equally crowded with berths and the chatter of hundreds of immigrants.

They wandered down the corridor in search of a way up to the deck. Some areas were roped-off, signs announcing penalties for any passenger who dared to cross. Finally Aatu found the steep, ladder-like steps leading up through a narrow opening. Soon the steerage deck was packed with passengers trying to catch one last glimpse of England. The crisp morning air blew across the deck, whipping at their cheeks, coloring them a rosy hue. Even Aatu looked flushed.

"If I could stand here the whole trip, looking at the water and sky," he wished aloud, "then I would be a happy man."

"They say after we pass through the channel that the ocean can be pretty rough," Mr. Hayrynen put in.

"Let's not talk of that now, please," Reeta begged, not wanting to think about the perils of the ocean just yet. "I'm starting to get hungry. Do you think the food will be any better here than on the other ship?"

Her question was answered presently. They were assigned to one of several dining halls on the steerage level. The setup was only slightly different. Here the passengers were seated at long tables first. Then meat and vegetables were placed on the tables in large tins that resembled dishpans.

"Where are the serving spoons?" Sonja asked, looking around.

"Seems we're supposed to use our own," Reeta said, gesturing to neighboring tables where the people were dipping into the large pans with whatever they had, spoon or cup.

"Guess we can forget the table manners," Aatu joked, reaching for the meat with his small spoon.

"And the Lord, too?" Reeta asked, poking him with her elbow.

"Oh, of course not," he apologized, setting the spoon down and bowing his head. He prayed loud enough so Reeta could hear.

When he had finished, Reeta looked up, noticing that a few families scattered here and there across the noisy dining hall were offering thanks also. Children peeked from behind laced fingers, waiting for the "Amen."

Sonja volunteered her cup for Reeta to dish up her food. "Here," she insisted, "use mine. No sense getting your cup messy too."

Aatu coughed, choking on his first bite of stringy beef.

Chapter Seventeen

MARKING THE DAYS

Like the English Robinson Crusoe, Reeta wanted to note the passage of days somehow so she wouldn't lose hope of this voyage ever coming to an end. Even had she been inclined to keep a diary, there was no opportunity to begin now, paper or pen being unobtainable. She settled for carefully scratching marks with the tines of her fork on the bottom of the lunch pail, beginning with two the next morning before breakfast.

The second day began with a call for the passengers to line up for a medical inspection. Reeta's hands shook for fear of what further indecencies might be required of them. She had barely slept during the night, unable to block out the sounds of children crying, women's muffled screaming, and men shouting or laughing. She hadn't wanted to know what was happening around her, and burying her head under the blanket, she prayed that she would not have to make a trip to the washroom.

A steward made the announcement: "All passengers will form a line through the dining hall. You must have your medical inspection cards ready to be punched."

"Come, now," Sonja said, pulling Reeta to her feet. "See, the men will go first, and I'll stay right beside you."

"All right," she agreed reluctantly, "but I don't think I trust these people."

Sonja eyed the line of people moving toward the dining hall. "Look at them," she said, pointing. "The line keeps moving all the time. It's probably just a quick look to see that we aren't dying of some disease or something."

They joined the line, finally passing single file before a doctor who was leisurely conversing with another officer.

"He didn't even look at us," Sonja marveled.

"Your card," the chief steward demanded, holding out his hand impatiently.

Reeta handed him her card. He punched it six times, returning it to her and motioning her to move along. The same for Sonja. They looked at each other, both in relief and astonishment. So much for six days of medical inspection.

* * *

Four marks were scratched on the bottom of the tin pail the day it began to storm. Passengers were confined to their compartments, only moving to the dining hall for meals if they weren't too sick. Everything swayed back and forth, as if they were on a giant swing, though not as gentle as any swing Reeta remembered.

There was no stopping it either. Some men, occasionally even a woman, tried cursing. A handful tried praying, as did Reeta. She was certain she had confessed every sin she had knowingly committed and maybe a few extra besides. Children cried and puked in their mothers' laps. Aatu's face became as white as the mattress cover. He could only moan and roll around in his berth.

"Here," Reeta offered, "I brought you a little broth from supper. Could you try it?" She tried to lift his head so he might take a few sips.

"It's no use," he said, moaning and coughing. "I can't. Let me be."

She pushed his freshly rinsed lunch pail closer in case he needed it during the night. The smell of sickness filled the huge room. It was enough to make even the few well people sick. Climbing into her birth, Reeta looked over at Sonja sleeping. Neither of them had been terribly seasick yet, though she didn't know how much longer she could endure this.

Suddenly a whiff of putrid air passed by. Reeta grabbed for her blanket, holding it up to her nose to block out the smell. Taking great gulps of air through her mouth, she managed to calm herself. *Think of lovely, fresh flowers or Mother's bread*, she said to herself, closing her eyes. It was no use; she grabbed for her lunch pail, reaching it just in time.

* * *

Reeta had already made the seventh mark on the tin lunch pail when she realized the room was not moving the way it had been during the past few days. Even the air didn't smell as bad. Maybe she was getting used to it.

Aatu was able to get himself out of his berth without help, though he looked terrible. The call had come for another medical inspection. Surely anyone could see he wasn't well.

"Maybe the doctor will give you something," Reeta reassured him as they made their way to the dining hall.

But the doctor didn't seem interested in anyone's health. He stood by with a distracted, unconcerned look on his face as the passengers filed by, this time baring their arms to show where they had been vaccinated. The steward punched their cards six more times. Medical inspections completed.

"Don't worry, Reeta," Aatu reassured her. "There's probably nothing to be done for seasickness anyway. How about us going up on deck?"

The idea of getting out of the stale air pushed all other concerns quickly out of her head. "Oh, yes!" she answered. "Will they let us go up?"

"Right this way!" Aatu climbed the steps slowly, pausing briefly to cough, and then continuing upward.

The fresh ocean breeze was like a taste of heaven, Reeta thought as they stood, breathing deeply of the morning air. The sun shone on the Atlantic, making the waves sparkle innocently. Were these the same waves that had beaten the ship for days? More passengers were finding their way up on deck, many wrapped in the gray company blankets. The people looked half dead, but as the sun dried the deck, causing a mist to rise into the clear blue sky, one by one, they began to revive. The life, which quite nearly had gone out of them, was slowly returning.

"Reeta, I must tell you," Aatu said, sighing deeply, "when I was so sick, I really wanted to die. I thought surely I would. But I couldn't die. I couldn't let go until I had seen America. That's what kept me going. It wasn't the thought of my family, or God, or anything else, just seeing

America. Am I terribly sinful, do you think?" He looked at her for reassurance.

"Of course you're not!" she answered, putting her arm through his. "Don't you think the Lord understands our dreams? Anyway, it seems He's allowing this one to come true."

She shuddered involuntarily, feeling a chasm forming between them. Aatu's dream of America was so different from her own. He saw some noble ideal, one she hoped would not be shattered, while she was here because of another person. If Thomas had gone to China, likely she would have followed.

* * *

The morning Reeta made the twelfth mark on the bottom of her lunch pail, she noticed flakes of rust from the cheap tin falling off into her food. It was hardly cause to set up a fuss. But it wasn't just the tinware; it was everything…her hair, her skin, her clothes, the bed. Could the entire world be dirty, sticky, and disagreeable to the touch? She combed her stringy hair tightly into a bun, hoping it didn't look as bad as it felt. This was a far cry from the scrubbed orderliness she had known all her life. *Mother*, she thought, *I'm glad you can't see me.*

"Watch out!" Sonja yelled from her berth across the aisle. "Here comes the cleanup crew." It was a joke, but nobody laughed.

Reeta pulled her feet up into her berth so they could get by. One steward swept the aisle every morning, while another lightly sprinkled sand on the floor. Never were the floors washed or disinfected, even when someone had been sick. And as for their beds, no attention was given to them by the crew, nor were any clean covers available.

Aatu didn't seem to be concerned about these little discomforts. He had recovered almost entirely from his bout of seasickness, only feeling slightly less energetic. His cough had not improved, however. By some stroke of fortune, he had come to make friends with both officers and crew alike. This allowed him to make certain explorations of the ship that others were denied.

* * *

On the fourteenth day of the passage, Aatu came down the crowded aisle, flopping down in the berth beside Reeta. Still trying to catch his breath, he motioned wildly, pointing toward the ceiling above them.

"What is it?" she prodded. "Where have you been today?" She always relished his tales of strange, new discoveries.

"An officer took me on a tour of the second cabin part of the ship," he whispered, pointing upward again as if he had been to heaven and back. "You wouldn't believe the difference. For a few more markkaa they have cabins that sleep only two or four people. Their deck is huge…nowhere nearly as crowded as ours, and it's more sheltered from the wind. They eat in a dining room where the food is served to them on plates, not tin. It looks like real food, too, not the slop we are forced to eat."

Reeta could see he was getting worked up about the way they had been treated. She put her hand to his mouth, "Sh-h-h! It will do no good to talk of this."

"But, Reeta," he said, trying to control himself, "You could have been up there if I hadn't been so selfish and arrogant."

"What in heaven's name are you talking about?" she asked, wondering at the painful expression on his face.

"Jake offered to change your ticket for second cabin." he explained, berating himself with each word, "but I turned him down flat. That was when we were in England. I should have taken his offer. I had no idea it would be like this."

Reeta was stunned, questions flooding her mind. Why would Jake have done that? Where could he have gotten that kind of money? What did he want from her?

"Will you forgive me, Reeta?" Aatu begged.

"There's nothing to forgive," she answered sincerely. "I couldn't possibly have taken the tickets. Thomas did the best he could, and that's good enough. Now, forget it."

* * *

On a sunny Wednesday morning, Reeta joyfully scratched the sixteenth mark on the bottom of the rusty lunch pail. Today would be the day of liberation.

The biscuits served for breakfast that morning had been as hard and tasteless as a bit of carpet…moldy, too. Instead of complaining, however, the passengers had taken them up to the deck and made a game of tossing them into the ocean. For nearly half an hour the hard disks went sailing high in the air, over the sides of the ship, accompanied by resounding cheers.

Chapter Eighteen

SHADOW OF THE LADY

Aatu could not be persuaded to leave the deck since the first sighting of the shores of America. At noon Reeta saved some of her lunch for him, but he hardly noticed the food, munching absentmindedly on a hard roll while he stared at the horizon. The busy harbor was coming into focus, its ships, barges, and boats of all kinds flying the colorful flags of many nations. Slowly the ocean liner turned a little to the port side.

"Reeta!" he said, grabbing her arm excitedly. "Look!"

She looked in the direction he pointed, seeing nothing at first. Then, leaning a bit over the rail, she gasped. "The Lady of the Harbor! She's magnificent!"

Slowly the statue was coming into full view. The sole inhabitant of a small island, it stood proudly atop a pedestal which was itself a massive building. The afternoon sun caught the sheen of her hammered copper robe. One arm stretched high into the heavens holding a torch, a sign of welcome and liberty to all who passed by.

Sonja joined them, the crowd pressing in behind her for a better view. "They said she was grand, but this is utterly amazing," she whispered in awe.

"How do you suppose they ever managed such a thing?'" Aatu asked. "Can any dream a man dreams come true in this incredible land?"

The steamship was heading toward a wharf not far away now. In the background the city of New York rose impressively, its skyline painted with tall buildings. When the ship came close to the pilings, the crew immediately sprang to life, securing it with giant ropes, its passage come to an end. When the gangplank from the upper deck was secure, well-dressed cabin passengers disembarked, anxious to pass through customs and immigration. Reeta found herself looking for Jake in the sea of faces, but he was not to be seen. After some time, the cabin passengers were off, and it was their turn.

Still weak from his bout with seasickness, Aatu couldn't manage to hoist the trunk to his back. This time he dragged it awkwardly with one hand, Reeta finally picking up the other end. Once on the pier, the steerage passengers were not allowed to follow the cabin passengers, but were herded like cattle in the opposite direction, only to be loaded onto ferryboats.

Unlike the cabin passengers, who had walked freely into their new homeland, they were being detained for inspection on a small island in the harbor. Reeta was not naive enough to think that life was always fair, but to be treated so differently, all for a few markkaa, was humiliating as well as disappointing.

Aatu protested when a steward grabbed his trunk. "Wait! That's ours!"

"Don't make a fuss about it," the steward warned in a menacing voice.

It seemed all the larger pieces of luggage were being taken to the lower level of the ferry, while the immigrants were allowed to carry smaller items onto the main deck for the short ride. They passed back beneath the shadow of the lady, stopping at the docks of Ellis Island.

On the island, they were greeted with strange shouts and commands given by guards of some sort. Aatu was so tired from the long hours of standing and waiting that he could barely manage the smaller bags.

"Here, let me take one more of those," Reeta offered. "I can get it. Look! There's Sonja and her father. I thought we lost them when we boarded the ferry."

She started to get out of line to call Sonja when a guard shoved her back in place. The man's rudeness doubly irritated her because she couldn't understand what he was saying.

"I don't think these men like their job any more than we like being here," Aatu whispered, keeping an eye on the ruffian.

"Maybe so," she said reluctantly, "but that's no excuse for being so rude. Just because we don't speak their language doesn't mean we are stupid. That's how they act…as if we were dumb animals that need prodding with a stick!"

They stared helplessly at the towered, red brick building in front of them. Whatever mysteries it held would wait for the morning. An interpreter informed them that the inspections would begin tomorrow and they were to please follow him to the dormitory rooms.

At first Reeta balked, her feet refusing to move.
Weeks of travel with little rest had culminated in yet
another delay. Then she caught a glimpse of Sonja, waving
from her place in line. Sonja! Why, if they had gone
straight through today, she wouldn't have had time to say a
proper good-bye. She had been a true friend. Reeta smiled,
waving back.

Picking up her things again, she followed the line to
yet another large sleeping room. She soon discovered that
the delay just might be a godsend. There was a bathing
house with showers…200 of them someone said…a
laundry, a restaurant, and even a roof garden with a view of
the city. The showers were definitely first on the list.

When she had thoroughly washed away the grimy
accumulation of her travels, dressing in fresh clothing,
Reeta felt almost human again. She and Sonja visited the
laundry next, soaking and scrubbing their clothing to their
hearts content.

"I don't know about you, dear," Sonja finally
concluded, staring at the line of laundry hanging to dry,
"but I'm ready to eat!"

"Yes!" Reeta agreed, adding one more pair of
stockings to the line. "I suppose our things will be all right
here, do you think?"

"Now who would want our old rags anyway?"
Sonja asked, swatting at a dark skirt, frayed at the hemline.
"If they steal it, the poor souls, they are much worse off
than I. God bless them."

Reeta smiled, reluctantly agreeing that her clothes
would be no treasure either.

"Who knows what the styles are here anyway?"
Sonja suggested. "The first thing I can, I'm getting
something really stylish."

"Oh, is that so?" Reeta responded. "And you don't think we're in style?" Being stylish had never occurred to her until that very minute.

"My dear Reeta," Sonja said, putting her hands on her hips and flouncing about the laundry room, "wait till you see me in New York dress!"

They laughed heartily, enjoying a few more moments of silliness before finding their way to the restaurant where the men would be waiting.

Aatu met them at the door, leading them to a table along the window side of the room. Reeta's feet kept slipping on the polished floor.

"Whatever have they used on the floors to make it so slippery?" she asked, grabbing for Aatu's arm.

"It's not what they used," Aatu said, grinning, "it's what they feed you."

"What?" Sonja joined in, nearly falling over the bench as she sat down.

Aatu leaned across the table, whispering, "It's the food, Sonja. The man said that on the days when they serve prune sandwiches it's always like this."

"Prune sandwiches?" Reeta asked in disbelief.

"Have one," Aatu suggested, taking a napkin off the plate in the center of the table. There they were, indeed. Each sandwich consisted of two slices of bread with several plump prunes nestled between. "But do be careful of the pits. It seems people are in the habit of spitting them on the floor."

The prune sandwiches, along with a glass of milk, made up their supper. What strange people these Americans are, Reeta thought, still amazed at such a concoction.

After supper they all decided to make a visit to the roof garden before retiring. Climbing a flight of steel steps, their footsteps echoed in a dimly lit stairwell. Mr. Hayrynen pushed open a large steel door at the top of the stairs, allowing them to step out into the night world.

Reeta pulled her shawl a little closer around her shoulders. The air was chilly, a cool breeze coming from the ocean, but the view before her soon made her forget all other sensations. The moon was full, a golden disk in a velvety black sky. She drank deeply of its splendid rays and secret messages, sending her own back again. The city across the harbor was lit up like many little Christmas trees, lights flickering from street lamps and buildings.

"Sonja," Reeta said, almost whispering, not wanting to disturb the beautiful scene, "just think. This is your home. Are you afraid, even a little?"

Sonja kept her gaze on the city, its lights reflected in her eyes. "Maybe just a bit," she admitted. "Oh, but it will be a glorious adventure, don't you think?" She turned quickly, giving Reeta a hug.

"I'll miss you," Reeta said, returning her hug. She pulled away, suddenly remembering something. Handing Sonja a small piece of paper, she offered, "Here, I have the address in Washington where you can write to me. I want to know everything."

"And you must tell me what happens with you and Thomas. I want to know what you hear of that Jake fellow, too." Sonja said. "I'm dying of curiosity."

The men interrupted their good-byes, escorting them to the other side of the roof. There stood the Lady of the Harbor, glowing splendidly in all her evening glory, lighting the way to their new home.

Reeta squeezed Aatu's hand. "Only a little longer," she said softly.

He coughed several times, his hand trembling in hers.

Chapter Nineteen

ISLE OF TEARS

It was best they had said their good-byes that night. In the morning, the place was a furor of activity, Reeta quickly losing track of Sonja and her father.

Reeta and Aatu found themselves in a crush of immigrants waiting in line, climbing the staircase to the Great Hall in the Main Building. A man in uniform told them to have their health tickets ready to show the doctor when they reached the top of the stairs. Wrestling the baggage, Reeta held the ticket clenched in her teeth as she climbed the stairs.

On the landing, a doctor wearing a dark suit with epaulets and an impressive-looking, gold badge stamped the ticket with the official Ellis Island stamp, instructing them to take the stairs going down to the right into the hall. They passed through a maze of numbered passageways with iron-pipe railings, referred to as "pens," stopping only when the crowd of immigrants in front of them blocked the way.

Reeta's assessment of their treatment had not improved from the day before. She was certain that people with cattle prods would appear any moment to hurry them along, like cows to the slaughter.

Finally they were ordered to sit on the narrow wooden bench attached to the iron railing in pen number twelve. There they waited their turn for the inspection to begin. When at last the number on their pen was called, they formed a line, standing nervously before the grim-faced doctor.

Aatu must have seen the fear on Reeta's face. "I'll go first," he volunteered, stepping in front of her, "It's nothing. Watch this." He submitted to the doctor checking for signs of favus heads in his scalp, then scrutinizing his face and body for signs of disease or deformation.

It doesn't look too bad, Reeta thought, watching him. She noticed an elderly man just in front of Aatu. An assistant to the doctor pointed to the man's legs, marking his coat lapel with white chalk. She wondered if limping were a crime in America, a reason for rejection.

An interpreter broke in to her thoughts, speaking curtly. "Your papers?"

"Yes," she answered, "right here." She gave the papers to the man before the doctor inspected her head, face and hands.

"Move along," the interpreter ordered briskly when the doctor had completed his examination.

Reeta squirmed as the second doctor took a buttonhook, pressing it on her eyelid, rolling the eyelid back over the hook none too gently. It seemed he would never let go. When he released her, motioning her along, she noticed several people waiting in line with white chalk marks on their coats. The letters apparently stood for various ailments or problems

Glancing at Aatu, she saw a desperate look in his eyes and the white chalk mark on his lapel: TB. A uniformed official was leading him off toward some rooms on the left.

"The doctors want to check me more closely," he called to her. "Stay in line. I'll find you soon." He followed the officer into a small room, the door closing firmly behind them.

"Oh, God, please!" Reeta prayed, clutching at her throat, not understanding what had gone wrong. She didn't move for a few moments, fear binding her feet to the floor.

"Miss, you must stay with the group," an interpreter directed, standing at her side. "This way."

After looking back at the closed door, she reluctantly followed the others, not wanting to get too far ahead of her brother.

Another inspector wearing a badge began asking them questions about the moral character of others within the party. "Do you know of anyone who..."

Reeta wasn't listening to the questions. What did the chalk letters mean? What if they wouldn't let Aatu go on? She was so distracted, she was barely able to shake her head at the official's questions, hoping it was the right answer. Evidently it worked, for she was told to sit in the waiting area again, this time behind the registry desk. If only she could talk to someone, her worries might be more bearable. No one sitting in the pen seemed to notice her distress.

Aatu still had not appeared when her group was called to form a line at the desk. Each immigrant was questioned by the registry official for several minutes. He read off a list of questions, an interpreter assisting him.

"What is your name?" he asked.

"Elsa Reeta Wayrynen."

"Who paid for your ship's fare?" he questioned, this time staring at her with his dark beady eyes.

"Thomas Juntunen…my husband-to-be," she answered awkwardly. She had never said the word husband before, about Thomas that is. It sounded strange, unreal.

"Do you have a job waiting for you?"

"Well, no," Reeta said, trying to explain. "You see, we are to be married. Thomas and I…"

The official proceeded, "What kind of work do you do?"

"I…uh, I can cook and clean."

The interpreter said something to the official who wrote hurriedly on the paper.

"Is anyone meeting you?" he continued.

"Thomas knew the sailing date. He's expecting me," she answered, wondering exactly how he could know when she would be there. What would she do if...

"What is your destination?"

"Astoria, Oregon."

"Can you read and write?"

"Yes," she replied, thinking happily what great pride her father had taken in seeing to his children's education.

"Have you ever been in prison?" the official continued matter-of-factly.

"No," Reeta answered, wondering who would admit to such a thing even if it were true.

"How much money do you have?" he asked, looking at her this time. "Show it to me."

While the official and the interpreter watched, Reeta opened one of the small bags, reached down to the bottom, and fished out a cloth purse containing the few markkaa her family had been able to spare. She handed it to the interpreter who counted the money, announcing her financial standing to the man across the desk.

"Where did you get it?" he asked

"From my father," she replied, wondering if Mother had approved of his indulgence. Probably not.

After a few more questions, the official stamped a card, handing it across the desk.

"This is your landing card," the interpreter said. "It means you are officially admitted into the United States. Please step around to the other side."

She accepted the card, marveling at the meaning such a small paper could contain. Taking a few steps, she remembered Aatu. The interpreter was busy with the next person, so she proceeded around the desk, hoping to see him soon. She didn't care what he had told her, she wasn't going one step farther without him.

Setting her bags down, she stood on the landing above three sets of stairs. People of all nationalities, their voices mixed in an excited chorus, were hauling their bags down the stairway designated to them by more uniformed men. Several groups stood nearby, crying and hugging each other. One woman wailed hysterically, holding on to a young girl until they were pried apart. Everyone in their party was sent down the stairs to the right, except for the girl, who was ushered down the center stairway.

"Poor child," a woman at Reeta's elbow explained. "She failed the eye exam…has trachoma or some such. She's being sent back."

Reeta started to panic. She looked around frantically for Aatu. At last she saw him coming around the registry desk.

"Aatu! Over here!" she called, not wanting to pick up her bags again, but afraid to leave them.

He saw her and began working his way through the piles of baggage and people. "Reeta!" he said, his voice trembling. "Is it all right with you? Are you cleared to go?"

"Yes, look!" she held out her card for him to see. "But what did they do with you? Are you..." She didn't have to ask the question; she could see the answer in his eyes.

"No, I can't go with you," he said, hanging his head pitifully. "They say I must have tuberculosis...the coughing and my lungs." He struck his clenched fist to his chest, releasing a cry of anguish.

Reeta threw her arms around his neck, sobbing in protest. "It's not fair! They can't be right!" she exclaimed, unable to accept the cold edict.

Aatu hugged her fiercely, and then pulled away, holding her at arm's length. "You must be strong, Reeta. Don't feel so bad for me; I did get to see America."

She looked into his sad, tear-filled eyes. *Yes, you saw America*, she thought, *just like Moses. God allowed him to look at the promise land, but he couldn't go in. What is my brother's sin, God?* She wondered.

"Miss," a man in uniform addressed her, "you must move along. You're blocking the stairs. Let me see your papers." He reached for the card in her hand and pointed to the stairway on the right. Examining Aatu's papers, he directed him to take the stairway in the middle, leading down to the detention area.

"They say I must stay here for a week or two until another ship leaves for England," Aatu explained, his voice calmer now. "It has to be a ship from the same steamship company, you see."

"Tell Father and Mother I love them," she said, stifling a sob. She hugged him one more time, whispering, "I love you, too!"

They parted then, each taking a stairway to a different destination. Reeta grieved for her brother, for his lost dream of America and for his illness. She grieved for herself, too. How could she manage without him?

Thomas, she thought, stopping to catch her breath, *I don't know if I can do this. Maybe God is punishing me for being self-willed. Maybe I should turn around right now and go home with Aatu.*

She looked back up the stairs against the tide of immigrants entering their new homeland with happy faces.

Chapter Twenty

AMERICA MORNING

Understanding little of what was going on and too sad to care, Reeta let the moneychangers have their way. She held the strange-looking American dollars in her hands, stroking the shiny silver between her fingers. Examining one more closely, she wondered who the man was on the coin, his face frozen in a perpetual stare. Would he have cared about a poor immigrant turned away at the door of his country?

A sense of complete aloneness engulfed her, causing her heart to beat wildly, pulsing through her veins. It felt as though an iron fist were squeezing her chest, till she feared it would burst. *God!* The deserted feeling ached behind her eyes; her cheeks were aflame. Her legs, moving helplessly as in a strong current, pulled her down the stairs and along the paved lane toward the dock.

Neatly-clipped hedges lined the way, evidence of someone's careful plan. They reminded Reeta that her plans for coming to America were turning upside-down before her eyes. Would something else go wrong? For half an hour she stood on the dock, the numbness beginning to wear off.

It should have been perfect, this first morning in America. With the help of a cool, ocean breeze, the sunshine of a new dawn broke through the early morning fog. The women were hooded one and all, many in their gayest shawls for the entry. Dressed in their Sunday suits and hats, men guarded the trunks, bags, and baskets that had survived the long passage from the Old World. Children danced with anticipation, but unshed tears threatened to break loose as Reeta stared at the activity around her.

Whistles sounded their high-pitched screeches as the railroad ferries pulled up to the dock ready to take them to the train stations in New York City and New Jersey. Officials in the railroad company uniforms stood by each ferry checking tickets and tagging immigrants. Examining her railroad ticket, landing pass, and other papers, the man wrote on a tag: "Reeta Wayrynen, Astoria, Oregon." The tag, pinned to her coat, flapped in the wind like a little bird wing. She boarded the ferry in silence, nodding to another man who helped to carry her bags onto the boat.

When the ferry was filled, the shrill whistle blew again, a parting farewell to Ellis Island. Reeta watched as the red-bricked building grew smaller. People were waving from the roof garden; she waved, too. Maybe Aatu was there.

Reeta sat on the edge of the backless wooden bench, watching the city loom closer. She wondered why Sonja would want to live in a place of brick and steel, where people lived side by side or on top of each other in numberless windowed buildings. There were no grassy meadows to walk through, no forests to hide in, or cottages nestled cozily by a clear stream. She was glad Thomas loved the things she did. By the time the ferry reached its destination, she was somewhat cheered at the thought of the far-off valley in the hills waiting for her.

Transferring to the railroad was uneventful despite the bustle of the station. Long, sleek train engines with what seemed to be miles of passenger cars lined the platform, steam rising from under their bellies. Porters busily carried baggage, pointing the way to numbered cars, speaking strange words all the while. Realizing the uselessness of her own tongue, Reeta pointed to her tag when asked a question, eventually being directed to a passenger car whose destination hopefully matched her ticket. A dark-skinned porter reached out, helping her up the steps into the car.

Fathers and mothers, children, and a few grandparents huddled in little groups, reserving their section of the car. One young husband helped his wife, quite large with child, arrange a comfortable seat by propping pillows behind her back. Aatu would have chosen a seat near the front of the car, so he could be in a convenient location to talk to the porter or begin exploration of the rest of the train. Thinking of her brother sent a fresh wave of loneliness drifting over Reeta.

She hastily found an empty place by a window halfway down the aisle. Pushing her bags under the seat as far as they would go, she settled into the stiff upholstered seat, her feet dangling, not quite touching the floor. If she stared very hard out the window at the station's flurry of activity, if she concentrated very hard on some object, she might succeed. She might not cry.

Someone brazenly flopped down in the seat beside her, not bothering to inquire if it were vacant. Reeta didn't look. She couldn't talk to anyone as yet; the tears were too close to the surface. Evidently, whoever it was didn't mind her silence, for no greeting was offered, only a faint floral scent intruding upon her private thoughts.

Much clanging and jerking of the railroad car, accompanied by the shouts of men and the screeching of nameless iron parts, signaled the train's departure from the station. Reeta involuntarily covered her ears, trying to block out the noise.

"That's some racket, isn't it?" her seat partner asked.

Curious, Reeta turned to see who addressed her. She was the silliest-looking girl Reeta had ever seen. Bright reddish-orange hair, the color of a fiery sunset, fluffed out from under her headscarf in an unlikely halo. Cobalt-blue eyes and masses of freckles gave her an irrepressible appearance. Indeed, her face was more freckle than face, Reeta thought. To her surprise, the girl spoke Finnish.

"Hello, my name's Britta," the girl introduced herself, "Britta Silvala." She held out her hand.

Reeta politely shook hands, automatically liking this strange creature with the freckled smile. "Uh, Reeta Wayrynen," she finally managed. "I'm sorry. I didn't mean to stare."

Britta laughed understandingly. "With a face like this, believe me, I'm used to it. It used to bother me. When I was little I tried scrubbing them off, but I've learned to use this face to my advantage. No one forgets me, if you know what I mean!"

Reeta smiled, realizing it wasn't a difficult thing to do after all. *Lord, you sent her, didn't you?* she thought, never before having imagined an angel with red hair.

Britta leaned over looking at the tag on Reeta's coat. "Astoria!" she exclaimed excitedly. "That's the very place

I'm going. How wonderful! My aunt and uncle live there. He's into hotels, owns them all over the country."

"You're going to live with your aunt and uncle?" Reeta asked, immediately thinking better of it. She shouldn't be so nosy. "I'm sorry. That's really none of my business."

"I don't mind," Britta smiled, her freckles crinkling into laugh lines. "It's no secret or anything mysterious. I've been living with my father, you see. He's a wanderer, never staying in one place very long. So, everyone decided I'd be better off with Aunt Kiki and Uncle Uuli. I guess they must be right, don't you think?"

"Of course," she assured her, having no idea what life would be like wandering the face of the earth. She had already had more than enough of such adventure. Reeta thought the young girl could be no more than thirteen or fourteen, but her eyes reflected a mysterious excitement and an intriguing worldliness.

The porter interrupted the conversation making a request, fully expecting they should understand. He leaned against the aisle seat, steadying himself as he train rattled along.

Britta handed over her ticket to the man, who seemed satisfied, giving it a punch with a shiny silver instrument. Reeta pulled a bag from under the seat and fumbled for her papers also. The ticket was nowhere to be seen. Reeta imagined herself being thrown off the train like so much trash.

"I just had it here somewhere," she said, pulling things from the bag a handful at a time. When she had emptied the bag's contents in her lap, she stood up, turning around to dump the whole lot into the seat.

The porter waited in the aisle, tapping the punch against the palm of his hand, rolling his eyes this way and that, but offering no help.

Certainly this was the trouble she had imagined would come.

"What's this?" Britta asked, pulling at the corner of something sticking out of Reeta's coat pocket. Smiling, she held up the missing ticket between her delicate fingers.

Punching the ticket, the porter shoved it at Reeta and continued up the aisle, mumbling to himself.

"Thanks," she said, rearranging the things in her bag.

"Say, how about something to eat?" Britta suggested. "I have an apple left. I bought it at the station. See?" She held up the first piece of fruit Reeta had seen in a very long time, aside from the plums of Ellis Island.

"You go ahead," she said reluctantly, "I wouldn't want to take your lunch."

"I insist. Here," Britta offered, placing the apple in her hand. "You just eat as much as you like, and I'll finish it off."

The offer was too tempting. She sank her teeth into the juicy red fruit, relishing the tart flavor. It was heavenly, she thought.

The clacking of the train moving over the iron rails sounded in a steady rhythm as the country passed by outside the window. With the jostling of the car, Britta's tongue seemed to have loosened also. Not that she had been reticent to talk before, but now she gushed with opinions, comments, news, and just plain talk about everything, throwing in an occasional question to be sure her audience was listening.

Reeta ate the apple, stopping as nearly as possible to the halfway mark, leaving neat rows of rippling teeth marks in the red skin. Britta accepted the remaining half matter-of-factly, hardly pausing in her continuing saga. Lulled by the rocking of the railroad car and the soothing friendly voice of her new friend, Reeta began drifting-off to sleep, her head slumping over to one side.

Chapter Twenty-One

TRAIN TALES

"Ps-s-st! Are you awake?"

The whisper startled Reeta from her dream. She had been in the little valley, the fruit trees in bloom. Thomas had been there. At least she had felt his presence. She was certain he would have appeared at any moment, but she had been abruptly yanked away.

"I almost saw him," she said aloud, still not opening her eyes.

"Reeta, I need to ask you to do me a big favor," begged Britta, leaning closer. "Are you awake?"

"Yes, I think so," she answered, yawning. Gradually the cobwebs cleared from her mind, and she realized she was on the train, far from her dreamed-of destination.

"Please, listen to me," Britta begged. "You've got to believe me! There's someone following me."

Reeta sat up, suddenly wide-awake. She looked into the girl's frightened eyes. "I'm listening," she said, "but why would anyone be following you?"

"Probably because of my uncle. He's very rich, you know," Britta said, ducking down lower in her seat. "Maybe they want to kidnap me for ransom."

Reeta leaned forward, trying to see over the high back of the seat in front of her, but Britta jerked her sleeve, pulling her back.

"Don't look! They might see you and get suspicious," she whispered hoarsely. "I have an idea. You must say that you are my... aunt. That's it! Oh, please?"

Reeta felt uncomfortable. She couldn't lie, not even for this desperate girl. "Don't worry, child." (She thought she sounded strangely like her own mother.) "I'll try to help you, but I can't tell a tale like that."

Just then an agitated gentleman paused in the aisle beside their seat, looking at the people across from them. The porter stood behind him waiting. Turning their way the man stared at Britta, his eyes squinting from the effort.

"Ah, it must be you," he spoke, the words whistling strangely through his nose.

Reeta reached a hand protectively around Britta. "She's with me, sir. What is your business?"

"My business?" the man sputtered, seemingly losing control of himself. "This girl here," he pointed his finger accusingly at Britta, "has stolen a brooch from my wife. We will take her to our car and have her searched." He reached for her arm.

Reeta looked at Britta, who was cringing in fear beside her. The accusation couldn't be true. Though she had known the girl only a short while, she couldn't imagine Britta stealing "Did you actually see her take it?" she questioned the man.

"Well, not exactly," the man fidgeted. "But she was talking to my wife, and when she left my wife discovered the brooch was missing."

"And you decided to blame this poor child?"

"But..." the man threw up his hands in exasperation while the porter whispered something to him. He glared at Britta one last time, and then turned on his heels, disappearing up the aisle.

Britta pulled away from Reeta, leaning over to stare after the man. "He's gone. Thanks for speaking up for me."

"Telling the truth is the best defense," Reeta advised, feeling uncertain somehow about the situation. "You were talking to his wife, then?"

"Just trying to be polite...make conversation, you know," she said. "Doesn't pay to be friendly with some people, I guess."

Reeta didn't want to ask the obvious question. It might offend her, but it had to be asked. "You didn't take the brooch, did you?" She spoke in the gentlest, most non-accusing way she could.

Britta looked directly at her now, tears forming behind her eyes. "You think I would steal?"

"I had to ask," Reeta apologized. Saying no more, she drew the girl into the circle of her arms, rocking her gently in an effort to reassure both of them.

As the days passed, the incident was not mentioned again, Reeta enjoying the company of the feisty little redhead. The mountains and lakes passed by, soon giving way to the prairie and mile after mile of treeless flatlands with cloudless blue skies. A steady flow of conversation passed between them, except during the quiet night hours when passengers slept as best they could.

"If I can ever sleep lying down flat again, with my legs stretched out as far as I please," Reeta said wistfully, "I'll think I've gone to heaven."

"I think my neck has a permanent kink in it," Britta complained, trying to arrange herself comfortably enough to go to sleep. "At least it's not so hot during the night."

"Yes," she agreed, "just when I can't bear the heat one minute longer, it starts to turn cooler. Do you think we can get some water to wash with tonight? I'm so sticky."

"Why don't you go check out the situation first," Britta said, yawning. "I'll watch our things till you get back."

Reeta rummaged through a bag until she found her fast-shrinking piece of soap and a fairly clean towel. Making her way down the aisle to the little washroom at the end of the car, she grabbed the seats in passing whenever the car jerked. Finally she came to the door, pushing it open and stepping inside.

No one else was about this time of night, so she went directly to the basin. The water was tepid, neither warm nor cold, but it was wet. She dipped a corner of her towel into the water. Dabbing it against her face, it felt wonderful. Since she had the place to herself, she scrubbed every inch of skin that she could reach. By the time she was ready to go back to her cramped seat, she felt somewhat refreshed again.

Traversing the rocking aisle once more, she found Britta sprawled out over the entire seat, sound asleep. Hanging the towel over the back of the seat, Reeta gazed at the sleeping girl, who almost looked comfortable, a little smile crossing her lips.

Reeta didn't have the heart to wake her or move her over to her side of the seat, so she gathered the blanket and small pillow provided by the railroad company, settling herself on the floor with her head resting on the seat. It wouldn't be so bad for an hour or so, she thought.

The sun was already filtering through the window shade when she awoke, finding herself slumped on the floor. She got up quickly, glad that not too many passengers were stirring. How embarrassing it would have been to be found curled up like a cat on the floor. She was smoothing out the wrinkles in her clothes when she realized Britta was missing.

No one had put Reeta in charge of the girl or even asked that she watch out for her, but all the same, she felt responsible. During the long hours on the train, the child had shared many personal details of her life. In fact, since she had met Britta, Reeta hadn't had much time to think about herself. She had told the girl about her family and about Thomas, of course, but it seemed the conversation always came back to Britta's exciting adventures traveling with her vagabond Father.

By the time Reeta had straightened up her things, Britta appeared, dancing around merrily. "Reeta, I just heard that we should be coming into Portland this evening!"

"Why, that means we might be in Astoria...tomorrow?" she asked, hardly daring to believe her long journey was coming to an end.

The day was spent packing and re-packing the few bags she had been allowed to carry on the train. Reeta prayed that her trunk was in the baggage car. She couldn't remember seeing it since the ferry trip to Ellis Island. What was packed in it, anyway? She tried making a mental list:

Mother's new rug
Father's Bible

puukko knife for Thomas
Hanna's embroidered sheets
good Sunday dress
a carved candlestick
a floral fringed shawl
good shoes....

"Whatever are you looking so worried about?" Britta asked. "You haven't lost something have you?"

"No, at least I hope not," Reeta lamented. "I was just trying to remember what I have in my trunk. If it should be lost, it would be like taking away part of my life. There's no way to replace those things."

"Goodness, I know what you mean. One time when my father and I were in Sweden, we..."

Britta was off telling another story, but Reeta didn't hear much of it, her own thoughts crowding out the girl's babbling voice.

It was evening, in fact it had been dark for some time when the train whistled, screeched, and rattled to a stop in the Portland train station. Reeta had washed, putting on her last clean dark print skirt and matching shirtwaist. After buttoning her coat so it wouldn't flap in the way, she tied her scarf under her chin securely. Then she gathered her bags, starting down the aisle after Britta.

Immediately they were directed toward another train for the comparatively short trip by rail to Astoria. Settling herself beside Britta in a car nearly identical to the previous one, Reeta waited tensely for the train to depart. No matter how many hours it took, she was certain there would be no sleeping for her this night.

Britta, however, was fast asleep, her head in Reeta's lap, when the train pulled out of the station, beginning its nighttime journey to Astoria. As the hours passed, Reeta leaned close to the dark windowpane, hoping to catch a glimpse of lights or the outline of the country illuminated by the pale moon.

Details and worries crowded close together with her dreams as the train made its way along the Columbia River on the Oregon side. Does Thomas know where I am? Is he at the logging camp, or maybe at the farm? She wondered.

"He's over there somewhere," she whispered, searching the dark hills across the river. She put her fingertips to the cool glass. "I'm coming, Thomas. I'm coming."

Chapter Twenty-Two

ASTORIA GREETING

The bustling port city at the mouth of the Columbia River awakened to another day. It was a typical day for most people, but for a new immigrant like Reeta, it was a day unparalleled. The reddish glow of the early morning sky bid no warning for her, unlike the ancient sailor's superstition. Here she would meet Thomas. Here she would begin a new life.

Dropping her bags on the platform of the railroad terminal, she stood like an unobserved statue amid the noise of welcome. Families and friends greeted and hugged one another, the confusion of languages making no difference. The meaning was understood.

Bouncing to a standstill beside her, Britta looked about the crowd. "Somewhere among all these people are my aunt and uncle," she said as if it were a game or a great puzzle to be solved. "Do you think I'll be able to guess who they are?"

"Sounds like quite a job to me," Reeta said, trying to figure out what should be done first. "Why don't we go to the ticket desk inside and see if there are any messages?"

"Wait!" she said, pointing to a couple standing nearby. "What do you think about them? He even looks a little like my father."

Before Reeta could offer an opinion, Britta rushed over to introduce herself to the couple. They shook their heads in bewilderment, and Britta returned, shrugging her shoulders.

"What happened?" Reeta asked.

"Don't know for sure," Britta smiled. "They only speak German!"

"Nice work!" Reeta teased. "Now let's check on the messages." She picked up her bags, leading the way through the crowd. Inside the large double-doors of the station, they headed toward the desk at one end of the room filled with people, baggage, and commotion.

Railroad agents behind the tall counter were busy answering questions, trying to match baggage numbers with a pile of bags being hauled in, and selling a few tickets for the next train. Though much of the conversation was in English, to her relief Reeta heard a clerk speaking Finnish also.

"Excuse me," she said to him.

He continued to sift through a pile of documents at the desk, paying no attention to her timid introduction.

She stood on tiptoe this time, though it hardly did much to improve her stature. Still looking like a child, her head and shoulders barely reaching above the counter, she tried again, this time with more force. "Excuse me, sir!"

The clerk looked down at her, a conciliatory expression on his face. "Yes?" was his singular reply.

"Have you any messages for either of us?" she asked, indicating Britta. "My name is Reeta Wayrynen, and this is Britta Silvala."

"Britta?" came the excited inquiry from a woman standing beside them. She was a rather buxom, motherly type, perhaps in her forties. The feathers in her stylish hat flounced in a flirty little dance when she spoke. "My goodness, it must be you! You look every bit like your dear mother, God rest her soul."

Wrapping Britta in an enthusiastic hug, she immediately began chatting about family…names, ages, and whereabouts of people she knew. Reeta turned back to the desk where the clerk was searching through a stack of messages.

"What is the name again?" he inquired, holding up an envelope to the light.

"Wayrynen. Reeta Wayrynen," she pronounced the name slowly, her eyes fixed upon the small white envelope.

"I guess this is it," he said, handing her the envelope across the desk, and then going back to another stack of papers.

She held the envelope in her hand, staring at her name scrawled across the front. People behind her were anxious to have their turn at the counter, so she stepped aside quickly, still squinting at her name.

Something was wrong. The handwriting was not Thomas'. The only thing she could think of was that he must be hurt, or worse. She had heard of terrible accidents happening in the logging camps where there were no doctors. Her hands trembling, she tore open the envelope, pulling out the letter. Scanning the unfamiliar handwriting, she came to a stop at the signature: Jake.

In disappointment, she crumpled the note in her hand, wondering whether to stomp it into the floor or to tear it into little pieces. Thomas surely would have left a message for her. This was impossible.

Britta's aunt moved toward her saying, "My niece tells me that you have been very kind to her. Reeta, is it?"

"Oh, well, she has been a fine traveling companion, too. Thank you, uh..." she hesitated not knowing what to call her.

"Mrs. Rosberg," she introduced herself, looking at the letter Reeta was still holding. "Is everything all right? Did you get your message?"

There was little else to do. Reeta unfolded the note, saying, "It's not exactly what I expected. Excuse me a minute, will you?" She stood by her bags, staring at the signature one more time before reading the note. Yes, there was the wrong name laughing at her from the bottom of the page. Ignoring the impulse to squash the letter into a little ball, she read on.

> *Reeta,*
>
> *Since you are likely a few days behind, I thought to leave this note to tell you that I have gone ahead up-river on a mail boat to seek out my adventurous brother.*
>
> *I must see him about something important, and so, couldn't wait for you. I'm sure he will get in touch with you soon. Best of luck to you.*
>
> *Jake*

Reeta stood in the middle of the station, the note forgotten in her hand. Jake had gone ahead; he was probably with Thomas right now. It wasn't fair! She looked about her, bewildered. Now what was she supposed to do? She wanted to rush into someone's arms and just cry and cry.

It was Mrs. Rosberg who was at her side momentarily. "My dear," she said, trying to help, "I can't leave until I know that things are settled for you. May I help?"

Britta stood beside her aunt, not joining in the conversation. In fact, she looked nervous about something.

Reeta sighed, stuffing the note into her pocket. "I guess there must be some mix-up. It seems that Thom..." She couldn't even say his name without stopping to choke back the tears.

The motherly shelter of Mrs. Rosberg's arms opened wide without hesitation. Reeta found herself sobbing out the whole confusing situation to her. Britta listened without saying a word, only offering a brief sympathetic glance, then staring back at her shoes.

"Listen here," Mrs. Rosberg ordered gently, taking Reeta by the shoulders, "we will get this whole mess settled soon enough. But right now, I insist you come along with us. We've plenty of room; it's the least we can do. "

"I guess I will need a room," Reeta conceded. "If your hotel isn't full?"

"Hotel?" Mrs. Rosberg said, laughing. "My goodness! My house has been called many things, but never a hotel, though I must admit it feels like one at times." Turning to a porter, she indicated the luggage to be loaded in the buggy, saying someone would come later for the larger pieces. "I'm certain it will take some time to unload the baggage car and straighten everything out."

Reeta looked at Britta questioningly, but she turned away, offering no explanation. It must be that they didn't live at the hotel. Of course, if they were as rich as Britta said, why would they live in a hotel? Britta is probably embarrassed about my lack of knowledge in such matters, she thought.

Reeta watched in wonder as Mrs. Rosberg drove the buggy slowly down the boulevard. The port was tucked in against a glorious, shining river, opening its mouth wide as it ran toward the ocean. Shops with gaily painted signs offered a wide assortment of wares. They could hear the bartering sounds from the fish market on the wharf. Mrs. Rosberg even pointed out a public sauna, a true mark of civilized society in any Finn's estimation.

Turning on to a tree-lined street, the buggy started to climb up steeply. Here the view of the city and river extended even to the misty shores of Washington. "It is a lovely place, Astoria," Reeta mused aloud.

The buggy turned again, this time to the right, moving along a level road cut out of the hillside. They soon came to a stop in front of a large, white house with a covered porch extending its entire width. Ornate carvings trimmed the roof like lace on a collar, and a steep stairway led up to the house from the street.

"Here we are, ladies," announced Mrs. Rosberg. "Just leave your bags in the buggy. The boys will be happy to fetch them up for you. Come, let's get you settled in. You must be exhausted."

She led the way, walking briskly up the stairway, through the screened front door, and into the hallway. While she took their coats, hanging them on hooks below the staircase, several little heads peeked curiously around a doorway. She swiftly shooed them away. "Not now children. They need to rest first."

After directing Britta to a room near the stairs, Mrs. Rosberg showed Reeta to an attic guestroom on the third floor. Little pink rosebuds adorned the cream-colored wallpaper. How elegant, she thought, feeling the white iron bed frame decorated with roses too, these sculptured of iron and resting at the top of each post. A delicately crocheted lace spread covered the full size bed, and a soft, braided rug lay on the polished wood floor. A small bedside table, a bureau containing three drawers, and a mirror were the only other furniture. Warm sunshine filled the cozy room, passing through filmy white curtains.

Reeta hadn't realized how tired she was. The long days on the jolting train had taken their toll. After unbuttoning her skirt and shirtwaist, she dropped them wearily on the rug, barely having enough energy to pull back the covers and crawl in between the floral scented sheets. They welcomed her, folding her in their smooth, cool expanse. She stretched out, oblivious to everything around her. *Rest... I must rest for a while...*

Chapter Twenty-Three

THE PARSONAGE

The distinctive aroma of cardamom bread and freshly brewed coffee drew Reeta from her sleep. *Mother must have gotten up early*, she thought, rising to an elbow. Focusing her eyes, she realized she was not at home, but in the elegant house on the hill, little pink rosebuds swimming around her head.

She lay back against the pillow wondering how long she had slept. The sun was still shining through the ruffled white curtains. Recent events drifted through her head like a foggy dream. A soft knock on the door caused her to pull the covers up under her chin.

"May I come in?" came a voice barely above a whisper from the other side of the door.

"Yes, hrm. It's fine." Reeta called, trying to get the frogginess out of her voice.

The door opened slowly, revealing a smiling Mrs. Rosberg balancing a serving tray laden with wonderful-smelling enticements. "I'm glad to see you are looking more rested today," she commented, setting the tray on the bed. Picking up a delicate china cup and saucer from the tray, she offered it to Reeta. "Here you are…a nice dark cup of coffee. This should revive your spirits, I'd say."

Reeta accepted the cup gladly, breathing deeply of the rich black brew. After taking a sip, she asked, "Did you say that I look more rested *today*?"

Mrs. Rosberg chuckled. "Yes, my dear, you slept the entire day and through the night. You must have been awfully worn out."

"A whole day?" she repeated incredulously. "There are so many things I should be doing."

"Don't worry, there's plenty of time. Now eat up." she ordered. Going to the window, she pulled back the curtains, opening up the hinged pane to let in the fresh air. "There, that's better. You can see the morning fog lying on the river from this window. It usually means it's going to be a lovely day."

Reeta began with a plate of eggs and a thick slice of cardamom bread spread with creamy butter. She couldn't remember when she had eaten anything quite so wonderful, at least since leaving home. Mrs. Rosberg had braided the sweet bread, topping it with brushed egg and sprinkled sugar, just as her own mother would have done. But the things of home already seemed so far away, so long ago.

Mrs. Rosberg watched her eat, smiling at her enthusiastic enjoyment of the meal. "When you're done, there's a washroom downstairs. Take your time," she said, moving toward the door. "My husband will be home for lunch. He's been looking forward to meeting you. The children have also, but I sent them out to play this morning so you could rest a little longer."

"Thank you for being so kind, Mrs. Rosberg," Reeta said sincerely, trying to focus back on her present situation.

"Please, do call me Aunt Kiki. I'd like that," she suggested, smiling from the doorway. "Oh, yes, I nearly forgot. Your trunk is sitting out here. I'll have the boys carry it into your room for you later." Closing the door, the sound of her footsteps could be heard padding down the carpeted hall.

Relieved that her trunk was safe, she looked at the tray, deciding on one more piece of bread. "It's not that I eat like this every day," she said aloud, trying to excuse her indulgence, "but it is a day to celebrate."

When she had washed and dressed, having found a clean change of clothes inside the trunk, she decided that the very next thing she must do was to write some letters. Aunt Kiki had set out everything she would need: stationary, envelopes, pen and ink. Settling herself at the large dining room table, she began with a letter for Thomas. Deep in thought, she was startled to see Britta staring at her from the doorway.

"Hello there," Reeta welcomed, noticing again how quiet Britta had grown since their arrival. "Is there something wrong?"

"Have you been talking with my aunt?" she asked, moving closer. She played with the edge of the lace tablecloth, not looking directly at Reeta. "I mean, did you talk about, well, things I told you?"

"Not exactly," Reeta answered, wondering what she might be worried about. "She's been so nice to me, helping me to feel welcome. I really like her."

"I wanted you to know that things haven't been going too well for my aunt and uncle...in the hotel business," Britta whispered, looking around to make certain no one else was listening. "They wouldn't talk about it I'm sure, but Uncle Uuli has given it up and gone back to preaching. So if you wouldn't mention anything about the hotel, then they wouldn't have to be embarrassed. You do understand?"

"Well, of course. I won't say anything." Reeta agreed, thinking this was a strange turn of events. "Is that all?"

"I guess so," she answered, hesitating for a moment while she smoothed out the tablecloth. "Oh, maybe you shouldn't say anything about my dad either. They never did get along very well. No use stirring up bad feelings, you know."

"You have my word on it," Reeta assured her. "What are friends for? You can tell me the truth; it won't change our friendship. Now, don't worry." She reached over patting Britta's hand.

Seemingly satisfied, the girl smiled wanly and disappeared through the doorway, while Reeta turned back to her letter writing.

Dear Thomas, she wrote. *I am finally here in Astoria.* What she really wanted to say next was, Where are you? You should have been here! I need you! Come and take me away right now. Instead, she settled for, *There was no message from you, so, happily, a kind lady has taken me into her home until I hear from you.*

She wanted to tell him, I long for the time when you will hold me in your arms and I will be yours alone. But she decided on, *I can't wait to see you again.* Who knows? Eli or Andrew might read the letter.

Finally she explained about Aatu's heartbreaking troubles, asking Thomas to give the news to her brothers. She sent her love. *Signed, Reeta.*

The letter to her parents was more difficult to write. By the time they would receive it, Aatu should already be home with much of the news. She didn't want to make them worry about her, so she decided to avoid the detail about not hearing from Thomas, concentrating on news about the train and her new-found friends in Astoria. It wasn't a very long letter, but it would have to do for now. She hoped her mother would write. Was that asking too much? She wondered.

After addressing the envelopes, she was putting away the writing materials when she caught a glimpse of movement in the kitchen doorway. Looking up she found several eager, rosy-cheeked children staring at her. They tumbled through the doorway in a wave of excitement, a small chubby-faced girl pulling Britta along by the arm.

"Hi! I'm Anna." offered the child. "I'm three. How old are you?"

"Don't mind her," a towheaded little boy announced. "My name is Armas. I'm seven. And this is Lassi. He's four, but he don't talk so much." He indicated his little companion peeking bashfully at her from behind the safety of his brother's back.

"It's very nice to meet all of you," Reeta replied.

"You can see our baby if you be very, very quiet," explained the dimpled Anna. "She's sleeping now. Do you want to see her?"

"That's enough, Anna," interrupted Aunt Kiki, standing in the doorway from the kitchen. Then turning to her houseguests, she said, "If you wouldn't mind helping get the children washed up, I'll have lunch ready soon."

It was difficult to tell who was helping who get washed as the giggling Anna wiggled and splashed between Reeta and Britta. While the child was drying herself with Britta's help, Reeta turned to the boys.

"I can take care of Lassi," Armas, said defensively. "He likes me to help him, don't you, Lassi?"

The younger boy clung to his brother like a Siamese twin, his wide-eyed face confirming that it was so. Armas took the towel Reeta held out, tossing it over his shoulder until he needed it. He proceeded to wash his little brother's hands and face, then patting them gently with the towel.

Tears clouded Reeta's eyes for a moment. She could see the boys' mutual dependence so clearly in their faces. It could have been a picture of her own brothers, Andrew protecting Aatu when he had been so sickly. Poor Aatu! He had no big brother to care for him now.

The sound of shouts and happy conversation pulled Reeta out of her nostalgia. She realized everyone had gone, leaving her standing with a damp towel in each hand. After hanging it over a hook, she walked into the large, warm kitchen, finding the children draped around a tall, thin man wearing a dark suit and a broad smile. He kissed each child, peeling them off one by one, so he could greet his guest.

"At last we meet, Miss Wayrynen," he said, making half a bow and extending his hand at the same time. "I do hope this rambunctious lot let you rest long enough."

"Yes, thank you," she replied, thinking how much she liked his twinkling soft blue eyes. "We were just getting acquainted."

"But you haven't met this one!" announced Aunt Kiki proudly, holding out the baby of the family for her inspection. "Her name is Kaarina."

A bundle of wiggles topped off with carrot-red hair squirmed in her mother's arms until she had to set her down. She toddled the few steps to her father, her chubby legs comically uncoordinated.

"Hello, Kaari!" he said, welcoming the child into his arms with a squeeze as he lifted her up for a kiss.

Soon they were all seated around the lunch table, little heads bowed as their father said grace. The moment he finished, lively conversation began again, only interrupted by mouthfuls of steaming soup and puffy, brown rolls.

"Where did you get that brooch?" Rev. Rosberg inquired, pointing to a lovely sparkling ornament pinned at the neck of his wife's dress.

"Oh, yes! Isn't it wonderful?" she answered, lovingly touching the brooch. "It's a present from Britta. It belonged to my sister. Wasn't that nice of her?"

Reeta stared at Britta...a cold, hurt stare.

Chapter Twenty-Four

MESSAGE RECEIVED

Rev. Rosberg offered to post the letters for Reeta on the way to his afternoon visitations--a new family in the church and an elderly widow who had been ill for some time. "It's no trouble at all," he insisted. "I'll check to see if there are any messages for you, too, while I'm there."

Reeta nodded, not wanting to hope too much for fear of disappointment. In fact, she was feeling rather depressed about life in general. Why were things never as simple as they seemed? She loved her parents and they loved her, yet they couldn't help hurting each other. Poor, innocent Aatu had done no wrong, but was denied his dream by a quirk of fate that he couldn't change. Thomas loved her, yet trials had separated them, holding them apart even now. Then there was sweet, lively Britta who was not the simple child she appeared, but held some secret tragedy deep inside herself, or so Reeta feared. What could have caused her to be deceitful? Had she spoken the truth at all?

"There's no sense in your sitting around looking unhappy," Aunt Kiki said, interrupting her bout with self-pity. "Why don't you come to the market with me? Britta can watch the children for an hour."

Reeta looked at Britta, hoping for some sign of remorse or the slightest twinge of guilt, but there was nothing. Her eyes seemed distant and hard beyond her years.

"Is that all right with you?" Aunt Kiki asked, clearly expecting an affirmative reply.

Britta shrugged her shoulders, avoiding an answer by turning to pick up Kaarina. "It looks like you and I are going to get acquainted, huh?" she said pulling her close to her cheek, their red hair mixing perfectly into one mass of curls.

In a few minutes Aunt Kiki had given orders to the children, gathered her shopping bag, pocketbook, and shawl, and ushered Reeta out the front door. The view from the porch was unclouded, overlooking the city, the wide river, and hills in the distance. As they walked down the steep stairway and then along the street toward town, they kept up light conversation about the city and various points of interest.

"I hope you don't mind walking," Aunt Kiki apologized. "I rather enjoy it myself."

"It's fine with me," Reeta said, feeling better with each breath of the warm afternoon air. She decided to take this opportunity to ask about Britta, not knowing when she would get the chance again.

"Your niece seems to like the children, and they've taken to her, too, I think. It should be good for her to live in a home like yours after..." She stopped there, remembering her promise not to bring up Britta's father or the hotel business.

"Yes, poor child, being left an orphan at any age is a tragedy," she sympathized.

"An orphan? I didn't know," Reeta stumbled over the revelation.

"Her dear mother, my sister, raised Britta alone until she died this year from a weak heart, the doctor said. She managed the best she could after Britta's father deserted them when she was quite small. She never really knew her father."

The words came in a shocking wave. So Britta had lied about her family, too. Things were beginning to make sense now. It wasn't necessary to tell her aunt about the wild stories. That had probably been Britta's way of covering the hurt of not having a father, Reeta decided. But the brooch! That was another thing altogether.

"And you say the brooch Britta gave you is your sister's?" she asked, hoping to hear some proof that it was truly so.

"Why, yes," Aunt Kiki said, suddenly stopping beneath a large shade tree to catch her breath. She looked at Reeta inquisitively. "Why do you ask?"

"No reason," she replied, trying to think of a way out gracefully. "It's...so lovely. I thought it must have been in your family, your mother's perhaps."

"Goodness, no!" she exclaimed, relinquishing the shade for the sunny sidewalk again. "My parents were quite poor. All their lives, they struggled at farming a small piece of land, barely able to make ends meet. Being a pastor's wife for nearly ten years is rich in comparison."

"Your husband has always been a pastor then?" Reeta asked, knowing the answer.

"Yes, he's known from the time he was a boy that God's call was on his life," she confided, a smile playing across her lips. "He wouldn't be happy doing anything else, and neither would I. I hope you and Thomas feel that way about your place in life. We've seen so many unhappy people, people trying to find something that can only be found in submitting to God's loving plan for their lives."

"And Britta..." began Reeta.

"She is just a child," she said firmly, fingering the brooch at her neck, "a very confused and hurt child. I'm hoping we can help her somehow, show her enough love."

They walked again, Aunt Kiki leading the way to her favorite haunts in the marketplace. The conversation turned to markets, and fish, and bread, the ordinary things making up their common experiences. No more was said of Britta, but Reeta felt no urgency to speak further on the matter. Aunt Kiki was nobody's fool.

When they returned home, carrying fresh vegetables and fish, Aunt Kiki stopped at the stairs. "That's strange," she said, pointing to the buggy on the street. "I wonder why Uuli is home so soon. You've no idea how he loves to talk. Sometimes his visits with parishioners take all afternoon." Looking up the stairs, she squinted, shading her eyes from the afternoon sun.

"Here, I'll carry the bag the rest of the way," Reeta offered, taking it from her. "You go on ahead and see what's happening."

"Thanks," she said, climbing up the stairs with a fresh burst of energy.

Reeta, however, not used to such hills, found the climb left her gasping for air. Reaching the top step, she sat down on the porch, trying to regain normal breathing before taking the bundle into the kitchen.

Staring down at the street and the buggy, she hoped there was nothing wrong. Rev. Rosberg could be home for any number of reasons. Maybe the people he'd planned to visit weren't at home, or maybe he'd simply forgotten something he should have taken with him. Then again, maybe someone had died or he had heard some terrible news. What if he had learned something about Thomas when he went to post her letters?

She heard the screen door behind her squeak as it swung open onto the porch, then returned back in its place with a bang. A current of cool air touched her neck as she sat up, her back pulled taunt and her heart beating in her throat.

Footsteps sounded, clump-clumping toward her across the porch. She could see from the corner of her eye the polished black shoes standing off to the side behind her. Breathing deeply, she was sure her suspicions were right. There must be bad news, and Rev. Rosberg was trying to think of a way to break it to her gently.

Reeta closed her eyes, swallowing back the unbidden tears. She waited, but he didn't speak. Instead, she sensed his movement closer to her. Opening her eyes, she saw he had come to stand beside her.

"Yes?" she spoke, still not looking up into his face, hardly able to bear the thought of what he might have to tell her.

"Reeta!" came the gentle reply, whispering softly through the warm afternoon.

The word sent a tremor through her heart. She leapt to her feet, dropping the bag of groceries on the porch. Carrots and potatoes rolled after each other about her feet as she stared at him. Him with his starched white collar slightly askew and his suit somewhat rumpled!

"Thomas!" she exclaimed, bursting into tears.

How could she be so desperately happy and at the same time cry with such wrenching sobs? She marveled at the paradox as he held her in his arms, both consoling her and, at the same time, weeping himself.

"At last, at last," he whispered in her ear, his voice shaking with emotion.

"Oh, God! Thomas!" she gasped, hardly believing her senses. "It's really you! How did you know I was here?"

"Do you have any hugs left for us?" asked a voice behind the screen door. Pushing the door open wide, her brothers stepped onto the porch, both of them grinning broadly.

"Eli! Andrew!" Reeta greeted each of them in turn, and then stood back reveling in the presence of her loved ones. "You must tell me how you found me. I mailed a letter to you only this morning."

"Oh, yes," Thomas nodded, pulling the envelope from his suit pocket, "you mean this one?"

"Now that is the best mail service time I've ever seen." Andrew said, his eyes opening in mock amazement.

"Then you know about Aatu?" she asked, fresh disappointment creeping into her heart. She looked at the city stretching out before them. "He should have been here; he wanted to come to America so badly."

Thomas took her hand in a gesture of sympathy. No one spoke for a few moments.

"Maybe Mother and Father need him at home," Eli suggested. "Losing the three of us at once has been hard on them, you know."

Shaking herself out of the solemn mood, Reeta looked at Thomas, remembering her question. "Tell me how you found me."

"Well, when Jake showed up, he had quite the story to tell. He said that he was sure you would be only a couple days behind him," he explained. "So we decided to come here and track you down. Then we met Rev. Rosberg at the station, and here we are."

"It sounds like Providence to me," she concluded, "except maybe for the part about Jake. I don't quite know what to make of that brother of yours. Where is he anyway?"

Thomas looked at Eli and Andrew with a strange camaraderie. Then, turning to her, he spoke decisively. "That is something we need to talk about…alone."

Chapter Twenty-Five

JAKE'S SHADOW

They walked together hand in hand, heading south up a steep street which offered an even larger panorama than had the parsonage porch. The late afternoon sun warmed them as it baptized the city in its golden light. Finding a vacant lot, Thomas took her arm, leading her through the tall, summer grasses to a fallen log. There he lifted her up to a fine view seat, climbing up beside her.

Unable to wait a moment longer, Reeta hugged his arm, saying, "Now, what did you need to tell me privately, and when can we leave for the farm? Rev. Rosberg is willing to marry us any time." She tried to see his face, but he was staring up the river, not yet ready to speak. "Thomas! What's wrong?"

He faced her reluctantly, an agonized expression coming over him. "Remember I said there was something about Jake?"

"Yes, but what does that have to do with our plans?" she asked, not really wanting to hear the answer. "No matter what Jake has done, it doesn't change our love for each other, does it?"

"Of course not!" he assured her, moving his arm around her shoulders. "But you don't know Jake very well, and I guess I didn't realize how far he might go to get what he wants."

She shivered at his words, not yet comprehending what Jake could have done to spoil things.

"When he arrived at the logging camp looking for me," Thomas confessed, "I was so surprised to see him that he threw me off guard with his talk and wild schemes."

Reeta listened, knowing that her apprehensions about Jake were about to take on reality. Could she have done something to stop him? Self-condemnation tied her tongue.

"He said he wanted to invest money in a business deal he'd cooked up. I told him right at the beginning that it was impossible, that I couldn't help him. He knew every cent I had was tied up in building the house." Thomas lowered his head, his voice shaking with disgust as he continued. "He wouldn't listen to reason, and he said I was selfish and had no family loyalty."

"But you didn't let him have the money?" she asked, praying he hadn't weakened.

"No," Thomas hesitated, then blurted out the horrible thing that had been burdening his soul. "He found out where I kept the money. He stole it! From his own flesh and blood!"

Reeta gasped, her face turning pale. "He stole the money for our house?" she managed to say at last. "How could he do that?"

"Oh, he left a note saying it was just a loan and that I shouldn't be angry because I'd get a big profit...later. But now, the money is gone to pay the laborers even for what's been done, and I can't purchase the supplies to complete the house either." Thomas wrung his hands helplessly, not wanting to go on. "That means there will be no place for you to come, Reeta. There are only a few small outbuildings, nothing good enough to live in for the winter."

She held on to his sleeve, clutching it as if he might vanish in the awful reality of his words. "We could make do somehow, couldn't we? There must be a way. Thomas, I can't let you go without me! Please!"

"There is nothing either of us can do about it," he spoke in a decisive voice. "I will not take you into the woods without building a proper home for you first, one your father would approve of. You must stay here until I can raise the money."

"No!" she protested, pulling away from him. "I won't stay here without you!"

"But you will." he said. "You must do this. I promised your father!"

Her dream valley in the hills was shrinking quickly out of her grasp. Thomas wouldn't even be with her; he was a fading dream, too. But Jake's phantom-like figure loomed grotesquely real, taunting and teasing her. She had never truly hated anyone in all her years, but now she knew the feeling. It was growing inside her.

"I'll be working in the woods as long as the weather holds, so you would have to be alone on the farm, anyway," Thomas reasoned. "I'm sure Rev. and Mrs. Rosberg could use some help in trade for your room and board here. I want us to be together as much as you do, but we must be patient. We must do this right. It's the only reasonable thing to do."

Reasonable? She didn't want to be reasonable. She wanted to be Mrs. Thomas Juntunen. She wanted to go home, to their own home. She wanted what she could not grasp.

Wilting against his shoulder, she felt the strength gone out of her. He held her tenderly for many minutes, neither of them speaking. The warm afternoon had begun its passage into evening, sending a chilly breeze up over the hill. Still they sat, lost in dreams gone sour.

"I wish we never had to leave this very spot," Reeta said, gazing over the city. She pointed across the road to a small whitewashed house. "See the windows of that house, the way the lights flicker orange and yellow through the curtains? Can't you just imagine the people inside sitting around a table, enjoying their family?"

"There will be a time for us, too," he spoke softly. "I must tell you that when I asked you to be my wife, I thought I loved you as much as a man can love a woman. But now, seeing you again and knowing what you are sacrificing for me, well, I think I didn't know very much about love at all."

"I don't understand how God could love us and do this!" Reeta cried out. "I mean, how could He lead us this far and then let Jake ruin things? Did we do something wrong?"

"Maybe if I had gone to school longer or listened better to the pastor's sermons, I could tell you the answers. Let's don't presume to know better than our Maker. There must be a reason behind it all." Thomas stood to his feet, a resolute stiffness in his back. "One thing I do know, however, is that we'd better start moving before they come looking for us."

They walked slowly back down the steep hillside to the road and the parsonage. Neither spoke much, being weighed down with heavy thoughts and with the agony of their situation.

When they arrived back at the house, Mrs. Rosberg had already put the extra leaf in the large walnut dining room table. Everyone seemed busy with a particular task. Even little Anna was carrying the spoons to each place, setting them down as carefully and straight as any three-year-old could.

The meal was special, though when she thought about it later, Reeta couldn't remember what had been served. The spirited conversation across the table and the happy faces of the people she loved cheered her soul. When the meal was finished, the men lingered at the table drinking coffee while the children were taken off to bed. Except for Armas.

"I'm almost eight! Isn't that old enough to stay and listen to the men talk?" Armas begged. "Please?"

His father smiled, saying, "It's fine with me, but you'd better check with your mother."

Mother agreed, so he stayed, listening to the grown-up's talk and gazing wistfully at the black coffee they seemed to enjoy so much.

Reeta helped Britta clear the table while Aunt Kiki refilled the cups. She brought in an extra cup, pouring a little of the dark brew in first, then adding twice as much cream and a heaping spoonful of sugar. Stirring it until the colors swirled and blended together, she placed it in front of Armas. He sat up as tall as he could, smiling a thank-you at his mother. Reeta hoped she would remember that picture when she had boys of her own.

In the kitchen, the clean-up went quickly with so many hands. Britta excused herself to go to her room, but before Reeta could go in to join the men, Aunt Kiki pulled her aside.

"Listen, dear," she began in a secretive voice. "I know your plans have been delayed, and I want you to know that I'd be happy, that is, *we'd* be happy to have you stay on here. Lord knows I could use help with the house and the children."

"That's very kind of you," she answered, sighing and knitting her fingers together nervously, "and I guess there is no other choice." Her shoulders sagged pitifully as she turned toward the dining room door.

"Wait!" Aunt Kiki said, putting a hand on her shoulder. "I have something else to tell you. It's merely a suggestion, you understand. Listen, why don't you and Thomas get married now, here in our home? We could make all the arrangements and have the wedding on Saturday!"

Reeta stared at her in surprise. "Saturday?" was all she could say. "That would be...tomorrow."

"Yes! Don't you see?" she questioned intently. "If you are married, it just might be the incentive your Thomas needs to hurry things along, to come for you sooner. So, what do you think?"

Married to Thomas. The words sounded wonderful to her ears, but this suggestion was so different from anything she had envisioned. "I...I don't know," she stammered.

"Let's see what the men think. After all, your brothers are here already. It's perfect!"

The conversation around the dining room table changed abruptly when Aunt Kiki surprised them with her idea. First they were shocked. Then excitement and reasons for and against the plan flew back and forth across the table.

Reeta hardly heard the discussion. The sound of it was muffled as if a great ocean echoed in her ears, rising and falling in roaring waves, not separate, discernible words. She stared intently at Thomas the whole while, hoping to see in his eyes what he truly thought of the idea.

After several minutes Eli and Andrew slapped Thomas on the back jovially, and the room grew quiet as his eyes met Reeta's. New hope sparkled in the gray depths of his eyes. It was like he was asking her to marry him all over again. Of course she would; no words were necessary.

"That settles it, then. Tomorrow it is!" Rev. Rosberg exclaimed, striking his hand on the table. He smiled broadly, as much to himself, perhaps, as to anyone there.

Tomorrow, she thought. Oh, happiest and saddest day of my life.

Chapter Twenty-Six

GLAD DAY, SAD DAY

By mid-morning the word was out. Aunt Kiki had contacted the head of the ladies missionary group, several deacons' wives, and Mrs. Poutanen, whose gossip network reached everyone that was of any consequence in the church. Reeta feared the sadly romantic story of the immigrant girl's wedding was quite likely embellished by the time the women had finished with it. But whatever the reason, the ladies of the church were eager to join forces.

They would see to it that this wedding was a proper celebration, food being of major importance in that respect. Aunt Kiki had no doubt that every lady of the Lutheran church was busy in her kitchen concocting some special treat for the evening, each trying to outdo the other. It would be a magnificent potluck dinner despite the short notice.

Thomas and Eli had disappeared on an undisclosed errand, but a group of the men, under Rev. Rosberg's supervision, were out hauling in borrowed chairs and decorating the porch with fir and cedar boughs they had gathered. Even Armas and Lassi helped carry and fetch as best they could. By noontime the parsonage was looking quite festive indeed.

Reeta sat on the floor in her attic room looking through the trunk. She pulled out her best dress, a pale green linen with forest green collar and cuffs. It would look perfect with the floral fringed shawl she unfolded and laid next to it on the bed. A good pressing is all it needs, she thought. She'd have to ask about the iron, but first, she reached for the gift from her father.

Holding his leather-bound Bible, she turned the pages lovingly, remembering the sound of his voice as he read to the family in the evenings by the firelight. In the front flyleaf were the names of several generations of Wayrynens, their births, marriages, and deaths recorded in ornate script.

Placing the Bible on her lap, she took a pen, dipping it in the inkbottle on the floor beside her, and then wrote: Thomas Juntunen ja Elsa Reeta Wayrynen, the sixth of August, 1907. To set the ink she blew gently on the page, fanning it with her hand at the same time. The ink lettering turned from shiny black to a dried matte finish, blending in with the other entries. After one final look she closed the book, setting it on the bed beside her wedding dress.

Pulling a small photograph out of the trunk, she gazed thoughtfully at the brown-tinted likeness of her parents. "I wish you were here today," she whispered. "You don't have to worry, you know. You would be proud of Thomas. Be happy for me, Papa."

Hearing a knock on the door, she looked up to see Britta peeking in. "Did you find the sheets yet? Aunt Kiki sent me to get them," she said with a sly little grin.

Aunt Kiki had insisted on secrecy about where the bridal couple would stay that night. She said it was her surprise for them. Even Britta, whose mouth was in continual motion, could not be persuaded to give the slightest clue.

"Just a minute," Reeta said, getting to her knees so she could sift through the things still packed away in the trunk. Feeling way to the bottom, she pulled out the sheets, delicately embroidered in a design of wildflowers and flowing ribbons. "Here they are. Did I tell you that my sister made these?" Turning around to hand her the sheets, she paled at the sight of Britta, standing near the bed with the open inkbottle in her hand.

"I'm sorry! I'm sorry!" Britta cried, a terrified look on her face. "I was just picking up the ink and...It was an accident!" She set the bottle on the chest, running from the room.

Aunt Kiki nearly collided with her in the doorway. "Gracious sakes! What is going on?"

Reeta still stood by the bed, Hanna's sheets clutched in her hands. There on the front of her dress was a dark blotch, black ink reaching its feathery fingers over the pale green linen. "It was an accident," she repeated Britta's words mechanically.

Quickly assessing the damage, Aunt Kiki grabbed the dress. "I'll put it to soak right away. I've got an idea. Don't worry!" She was off, flying down the stairs.

By the time Reeta came to her senses, still holding the sheets, she had followed the sounds down to the kitchen. Britta stood by the sink sulking while Aunt Kiki scrubbed at the ink spot, and then left it soaking.

Drying her hands she took the sheets from Reeta. "These are lovely, dear" she complimented. "Come with me. I have something to show you." They walked together down the narrow hallway to the end, where a small chest sat squarely against the wall between two doors.

Bending over Aunt Kiki lifted the lid, which squeaked and groaned before revealing its contents.

"Yes, I knew it was here. Look!" she said, holding up the most beautiful lace dress Reeta had ever seen. "It was my wedding dress. I want you to wear it."

Reeta couldn't speak. She felt of the silky, cream-colored dress, covered with a wide lace collar and insets of lace running down the sleeves and around the skirt.

"It will fit perfectly," she continued, holding it up to Reeta for a look before nodding approvingly. "Please wear it. It would make me so happy."

"If you're sure you don't mind," she said, hesitating. "It's so lovely!"

"Not another word about it," Aunt Kiki insisted, closing the chest. "Let's give it a little pressing and let you try it on."

Reeta tried to assure Britta that there were no hard feelings about the ink stain, but Britta pouted just the same. There wasn't time to set the matter straight with everything that waited to be done before evening. I'll talk to her tomorrow, she thought, carrying the borrowed wedding dress upstairs for a try on.

By the time the grandfather clock in the parlor struck six, the parsonage was filled with guests and well-wishers. The kitchen and dining room tables were piled with pies, cakes, and casseroles of every description. Women and girls fussed and fluttered about the food in their finery, while the men milled around outside and little boys chased across the yard, trying not to get grass stains on their Sunday clothes.

"We're ready for you. Reeta," called Aunt Kiki.

Picking up the bouquet of roses, fresh from the garden, she stopped at the mirror for one last look. She pushed a stray strand of hair back into place and pinched her cheeks just a little to bring out some color. Though she usually blushed easily, today she looked pale. Stepping out into the hall, her stomach wrenched suddenly, sending out waves of nausea. Maybe she would be sick.

Eli appeared at the bottom of the stairs, his hand stretching up toward her, ready to escort her out to the porch. "You look beautiful!" he whispered when she took his arm. "Thomas is a lucky man, indeed."

Together they walked out onto the porch. People nearby whispered their approval, but Reeta had eyes only for Thomas. He was standing with Andrew and Rev. Rosberg, nervously rubbing the toe of his shoe against one pant leg and inspecting the shine.

When he saw her, his mouth fell open slightly as he stared at her. She blushed in a warm flush that nearly matched the delicate reddish-pink of her bouquet. In a moment they stood side by side before Rev. Rosberg, who held her father's Bible and began the ceremony with a prayer.

After a brief exhortation to the bride and groom on the sanctity of their vows, he proceeded. "Reeta, do you take Thomas to be your lawfully wedded husband?"

"I do," she answered barely above a whisper, her hands quivering underneath the flowers.

"Thomas, do you take Reeta as your lawfully wedded wife?"

He reached out, taking her shaking hands in his own. "I do," he spoke steadily.

"Do you have a ring as a token of your pledge?" Rev. Rosberg asked Thomas.

A ring? Of course, but Reeta hadn't had time to wonder about it.

Thomas reached in his pocket, bringing out a shiny gold band. "It's probably too big," he whispered the apology, placing it on her ring finger, "but it's the best I could do for now."

"Try the middle finger," she suggested, whispering too.

He made the switch, the gold band fitting perfectly this time. They smiled at each other, and upon the minister's urging, kissed amid the whooping and applauding of the guests.

Eli was next to claim a kiss from the bride, followed by Andrew. From there the celebration began in earnest, the guests greeting the bride and groom enthusiastically with hugs and handshakes. Everyone seemed to love a good wedding, some ladies crying though they had never seen the couple until that very day.

Before the reception line had finished, several men brought out their instruments: an accordion, a violin, a couple mandolins, and, of course, the kantele, a small harp of five strings. Lilting melodies floated out in the evening air while the guests prepared to indulge in the generous display of food.

Pulling Reeta close to his side, Thomas whispered. "Mrs. Rosberg said we should meet her on the back porch when we have had enough celebrating. Are you hungry?"

"No, I couldn't eat a bite," she answered. "What's the secret?"

Thomas didn't answer, only took her hand, pulling her along as he squeezed through the crowded dining room and kitchen, then out the back door. Through the evening shadows a figure approached across the yard.

"Aunt Kiki!" Reeta ran down the steps to give her a hug. "You're such a dear! Thank you for everything."

"Here," she said, handing Thomas a lantern, and then pointing across the yard the way she had come. "Follow the path up the hill. It's not far. God bless you!" She disappeared into the house.

Starting across the yard, with one hand Thomas held the lantern high, and with the other he clasped her waist, leading her along the narrow path. Just past the first dense patch of trees a tiny house came into view, its only window lit up in welcome. A note tacked to the door simply said: *Enjoy.*

He pushed open the door, peering into the room where a small fireplace provided its flickering, cozy light, and a bed made-up with embroidered sheets stood in one corner. Then, sweeping her effortlessly into his arms, he carried her into the house kicking the door shut behind them.

She clung to his neck, saying, "Oh, Thomas, tomorrow..."

"Hush!" he whispered. "Today, be glad for today."

Chapter Twenty-Seven

MELANCHOLY

By Sunday morning the weather had changed, a cool mist falling gently over the city. It was the kind of rain that made everything new and fresh-smelling. It would straighten any curl left in her hair, she thought, wrapping the long brown strands into a loose knot at the nape of her neck. Standing just outside the door of the little house that had been theirs for but a night, Reeta breathed in the fragrance of the new day.

"How long?" she asked, hoping he would change his mind, but at the same time knowing the determination of the man she had married.

"An hour, maybe two," he replied, placing his broad hands tenderly on her shoulders as he stood behind her. "I wish things could be different."

She turned toward him, wrapping her arms possessively around his broad chest. "Please, Thomas!" she begged, "Isn't there somewhere I could stay?"

Not speaking, only sighing deeply in anguish, he held her. "My dear Reeta, don't you think I have tried to think of a way?" he chided. "It's just not possible."

She felt bad for tormenting him, but the thought of spending another year without him was too much to bear. Though she dared not speak the name, it was Jake that occupied much of her thoughts this morning. He had come to spoil their few hours together. She hated him. She would call him a selfish, egotistical thief right to his face, if he should appear.

Thomas reached out, cupping her face in his hands and gently rubbing his thumb against her cheek. "Don't worry so much. There must be a reason for this," he said, trying to convince her and maybe himself, too, at the same time. "It could be that we will treasure each other and love each other more than we ever could have if the way had been smooth." His eyes bore witness that he truly believed God was in control. "The same God who brought us together will keep us when we are apart."

She wanted to believe, but her heart was tainted with bitterness. To her, Jake seemed to have more control over their lives than God.

He bent forward, kissing her tenderly, then passionately while standing in the open doorway. When at last she gasped for air, they both stepped back, laughing. Ah, laughter was a medicine for the soul, she admitted to herself. Was that from the Bible? She thought so.

"We'd better got moving if we are going to get a little breakfast before it's time to leave," Thomas urged, though he didn't hurry. He slowly gathered up his things, slipping them into his small satchel.

The path back to the house was slippery from the morning's rain, so she clung to his steady arm as they descended to the yard. Andrew waved from the kitchen window, his smile visible even at that distance

Opening the door, Eli bowed slightly, winking at the couple. "Breakfast is waiting, Mr. and Mrs. Juntunen," he said most solemnly. "Have no fear; it was actually the dear Mrs. Rosberg who prepared it. They are all off to church, you see."

Thomas ate heartily, but she could do no more than push the food around on her plate while the men talked. The minutes of their life together were ticking away, and still the men talked. Finally as they were getting up from the table, Eli motioned for her to step into the hall with him. She followed.

Putting his arm around her shoulder, he whispered, "I'm so glad you and Thomas decided to get married. You'll be with him soon. Don't fret, little sister. And then you can help us celebrate our wedding, Sarah's and mine."

Reeta hugged him, truly happy for them both. "I'm so glad she has consented to be your wife!"

"Well, I haven't exactly asked her yet," he said, nervously twisting his finger through the buttonhole of his jacket. "But it's understood; she knows how I feel."

"A word of advice for you, big brother." she whispered seriously, poking a finger at his chest for emphasis. "Tell her before it's too late. She's a pretty young girl, and she won't be waiting around too long." Sarah seems like a sensible girl, Reeta thought, hoping Eli's plans would work out.

The mist was still falling when the four of them began their walk down to the dock where the small boat would be waiting to take the men on its trek up-river to Stella. Conversation was slow, no one feeling compelled to offer more than absolutely necessary. They were nearing the river when Thomas spoke quietly, "You'll be all right here?"

If he needed reassurance, she wasn't so sure herself. "I'll be fine," she answered, her voice lacking enthusiasm.

"You know if I don't go back today, I'll lose my job and our hopes for the house along with it?" he pleaded for her support. "Just tell me you understand."

She really did understand, but that didn't mean she had to like it. "I know, I know," she said, nodding.

The boat was preparing to leave when they arrived at the dock, the crinkled, old fisherman yelling orders to his small crew. Eli and Andrew quickly kissed her on the cheek and ran to make certain the boat would not leave without them.

Taking her hands in his, Thomas gently kissed her full on the lips one more time. She felt a warm flush in her cheeks, though no one was looking.

"I promise I'll come for you as soon as I can. I love you," he whispered before letting her go.

Heartbroken, she could only nod, watching as he boarded the small boat. Momentarily it pulled away from the dock, moving out into the main channel. She waved until the boat was merely a speck in the wide river, then letting her arm fall limply to her side.

The soft mewing of a seagull flying far away and the gentle lapping of the cold river against thick pilings underfoot were the only sounds breaking the stillness. Feeling the slick gold band on her finger precipitated the tears, flowing freely down her rosy cheeks. Alone. Not even the separation on Ellis Island seemed quite as devastating as this feeling now growing inside her quivering body.

She couldn't remember how long it had been or what route she had taken back from the river. Somehow Reeta found herself standing in the little attic room in the parsonage. Closing the door, she crossed wearily to the bed, flinging herself across its expanse and burying her face in the pillow.

For the next few days, Reeta walked about doing the things expected of her, but spending much of her time in the attic room brooding or pacing from the iron bed to the window and back. When the children asked her to do something, she did it with little enthusiasm.

Aunt Kiki seemed to understand her mood, trying to keep her busy. "Every week I'll need help fluffing up the mattresses and changing the linens. Armas always hated this chore," she admitted. "It's nice having you and Britta both in the house."

It's not that Reeta minded doing any of the chores assigned to her around the house, in fact, she was happy to be of help. Being a maid wasn't demeaning to her. She really felt more like a part of the family than the maid who, at the end of each week, received the small stipend agreed upon. She guessed that the irritation came from the fact that she wanted to do all of these things for Thomas, in their own house.

Fall had come with its fiery colors, turning the mornings crisper. Armas was in school, and Lassi was happy to entertain himself with a top or ball or exploring the small wood behind the parsonage until his brother came home. Britta spent most of her time running after Anna and holding baby Kaarina. It was clear the little girls loved her dearly, a fact Britta guarded jealously. Both Aunt Kiki and Reeta allowed Britta's indulgences with the girls, hoping she would feel accepted.

One evening in late October, a message came to the parsonage. A small child with a dirt-streaked face stood in the doorway holding out a wrinkled note to Reeta.

"Please, Ma'am," the tiny voice pleaded, "my mother needs some help. She said you would help!"

Reeta took the note from the child's trembling hands. The poor mother was a widow and didn't know what to do with her sick baby. Could someone come?

Aunt Kiki had been reading over Reeta's shoulder while she wiped her sudsy hands on her print apron. "We'll help, of course," she soothed the nervous child. "Britta, would you go with her right now? I'll be over as soon as I can gather a few supplies together." Already she was pulling off her apron, heading for the kitchen.

"Aunt Kiki," came the whining voice from the davenport. "I really don't think I should go." Britta leaned back against the tall back, moving one hand dramatically across her forehead.

Aunt Kiki turned toward her, frowning with disapproval at such a notion. "What?" she asked, her hands on her hips.

Britta had never before refused to do anything her aunt had asked. Even little Anna stared in astonishment.

Britta, however, was not intimidated. "I've had this horrible headache all day," she confessed. "I didn't complain about it, but it would hardly do for me to be around a sick baby now, don't you think?"

Aunt Kiki looked at Reeta, perhaps wondering what to do next.

"It's no trouble," Reeta said, reading her thoughts. "I'll just grab my shawl and be off."

She was out the door in a minute, the little ragamuffin pulling her along the street. After several blocks

they turned up a steep pathway to a dimly-lit house, more
like the size of the guest cottage where she had spent her
wedding night. From the street they could hear the baby's
plaintive howling. Once inside, Reeta took the wailing
bundle from the weary, little mother, who remained seated
in a small rocker while two other children clung to her. The
baby was beet-red from crying or fever. Which one it was,
Reeta couldn't tell.

"Get a rag with some cool water," she ordered the
girl, evidently the oldest of several children.

The mother nodded for her to obey, and she was
off, returning shortly with a dingy rag dampened with tepid
water from a pail. Reeta sighed, wishing she could offer to
take the baby to the parsonage until it was well. She'd
hardly had time to more than begin dabbing the baby with
the rag when heavy footsteps sounded on the porch. The
girl ran to open the door as it vibrated from the loud
thumping. An elderly gentleman carrying a black satchel
made no greeting, but came directly to Reeta's side.

"Thank God, you've come!" the poor mother
exclaimed, still unable to rise from her chair. "We were
afraid it might be too late."

She wrapped her arms across her chest, rocking
back and forth almost hysterically.

Reeta gladly stepped aside to let the doctor have a
look at the still-sobbing baby. Mumbling to himself, the
doctor peered and poked at the child for several minutes.
"No doubt about it, Mrs. Saari," he pronounced, looking at
her through tightly knitted eyebrows. "She's got the
measles! This house is quarantined; no one may leave."

Chapter Twenty-Eight

QUARANTINE

Protesting was pointless. She had been in the house; she had touched the baby. The doctor issued strict orders on care for the infant and signs to watch for in the other children. It could be a week or more, but they were likely to come down with the measles, too. Though fairly innocuous in some cases, measles could be very serious, especially for adults. People died.

She had little time to feel pity for herself. Mrs. Saari sat in a stupor, trying to take in the doctor's instructions, but too tired to comprehend much of what he said.

"Reeta, is it?" the doctor asked, seemingly assessing her capabilities as he spoke.

She nodded, knowing full well what he would say.

"I'm counting on you to make certain that my instructions are followed," he ordered, writing down some quick notes on a piece of paper, and then handing them to her. "I'll be back each day to have a look and bring anything you need."

"Yes, I understand," Reeta said, nodding again. She wondered how she could have let herself get in such a mess.

The doctor disappeared as quickly as he had arrived, leaving behind his note and a bottle of medicine. Reeta went to the window to see which way he had gone. There stood Aunt Kiki, talking to the doctor. He briskly ushered her back down the walkway, not even allowing her a glimpse inside the small house. Within the hour there appeared, nailed to the front door, a bright yellow paper warning that the house was being quarantined for measles.

First Reeta bathed the baby, her hot little body cringing at each touch. Then, opening the brown bottle of medicine the doctor had left, she dabbed the curious lotion gently on the baby's stomach covering the red blotches. The cool lotion soothed the child almost immediately. She was nearly asleep when Reeta wrapped her snugly in the ragged blanket, laying her ever so gently in the small cradle by her mother's bed.

Too exhausted to help, Mrs. Saari had fallen asleep, her frail body curled up, taking only a corner of the double bed. She didn't look much bigger than her oldest daughter. Pulling a worn blanket across the young mother's shoulders, Reeta tucked the corner gently under the thin mattress.

The sad eyes of the girl who had run through the night to get help stared at her mother. "She's...she's not going to die is she?" the girl asked.

"No!" Reeta answered, startled by the girl's question. "She's just very tired. We must all be quiet so they both can sleep. All right?"

The girl nodded, taking a few steps backwards. "Are you really going to stay with us?" she asked incredulously.

Not wanting to frighten the children with talk of quarantine, she assured her. "Yes, I'll stay with you as long as your mother needs help. Now don't you think you should tell me your names? You do have names?" she teased.

The brave little messenger was first to speak. "I'm Lina, and the baby's name is Marta."

As if somehow acknowledging the introduction, the baby flinched, her delicate fingers opening and closing like tiny butterfly wings.

"Marta," Reeta mouthed the name, thinking it had just the right sound. Then, turning her gaze toward the two little boys standing nearby, she asked cautiously, "And what are your names?"

In a single motion, both of them darted behind the rocking chair, peeking between the spindles of the tall back like two little birds in a cage. Large blue eyes stared warily as she stepped closer.

"The big one's Jacob, and the little one's John," Lina said, pointing accusingly. "They don't talk much, and they ain't much help!" She glared at the boys indignantly.

"Is that so?" Reeta remarked soothingly. She pulled the boys out from behind the rocker, firmly ushering them over to the window where she could get a better look at them. "I'd say there must be some handsome little fellows beneath these dirty faces. Lina, get me some soap and water."

Thus began the scrubbing and setting in order of the sad little house. One by one the children obediently submitted to the rag and a change of clothes, Reeta transforming them from wild-eyed creatures into clean, quite normal-looking children.

That chore done, Reeta realized there was much other work that had been neglected. Dust lay in wispy piles in every corner, cobwebs dangled precariously from the ceiling, and the small shelves in the corner where dishes probably should have been stacked sat empty, dirty plates scattered everywhere. Might as well make herself useful, she thought, trying to avoid brooding over the danger she might be in.

Each of the children diligently performed various chores as she assigned, trying not to disturb the sleepers. By the time Mrs. Saari awoke from her nap, the house was considerably tidier.

During the next week, Aunt Kiki left such things as they might need on the front walkway, first calling her greeting and then walking away before Lina was allowed to fetch the bundle. John and Jacob claimed the privilege of unwrapping the bundles, each of them taking turns pulling out welcome treasures: freshly baked bread, a jar of milk, or even a pair of socks knit especially for them.

The doctor stopped in each morning on his way to town. As could have been predicted, on the first morning of Reeta's second week of isolation, Lina broke out with the red spots, and the boys were acting crabby and out-of-sorts, too.

"They'll probably be next," the doctor surmised after feeling Jacob's forehead.

John refused to hold still, but crouched, whining behind the empty rocker. He broke out two days later, and Jacob followed suit the morning after.

"Three speckled baby birds in one nest," Reeta crooned, dabbing their itchy spots with the cool lotion.

Lina ordinarily would have risen up to protest such talk, but she was too sick to care. The rambunctious boys, only moaned and slept fitfully, complaining the light was too bright even though the curtains were drawn. Reeta finally nailed a blanket over the window.

No matter what the chore, even cleaning soiled linens or bathing feverish little bodies, Reeta neither complained nor considered that she should be pitied. So deep had the seeds of resentment for Jake settled in her heart, that he became the scapegoat, the one to blame for all her problems. It was Jake's fault that she was not in her own house with Thomas right now. It was Jake's fault she was a maid in Astoria. It was Jake's fault she was quarantined in this house with these sick children. It was Jake's fault she was so unhappy. So complete was her unspoken hatred for Jake, that she found herself confined in a prison more real than the small house itself.

It had been a month since that evening when Lina had come running up the parsonage steps for help. Jacob's spots were finally fading, everyone in the cramped little house anxiously noting his progress. She might soon be released from the quarantine. The idea flickered momentarily in the dark melancholy room of her mind.

The doctor arrived earlier than usual that afternoon, hopefully to make a decision about lifting the quarantine. He eyed the boys carefully, declaring, "Hmm...Yes, I'd say that we have about run the course. Looks good to me." Then, staring at Reeta, he squinted his eyes, speaking slowly, "Everyone else is feeling well?"

"Yes, thank you," Reeta replied, even managing a smile. Her eyelids felt heavy, probably from lack of sleep and the dim light in the little house. "We'll all be glad to get back to normal." What she missed most was the comfort of her own bed in the small attic room. Every muscle in her body ached. She wanted to lie down and sleep for a week at least.

Anticipating the doctor's next words, she rose quickly to her feet, standing near the small table where he was looking for something in his bag. The shiny buckle on the bag caught her eye. It sparkled strangely, suddenly bursting into lights that whirled wildly around her head. Then everything went black.

A cool rag touched her face in the dark. More blackness. Her mother stared at her disapprovingly, all the while giving a lecture about being careless. The words crackled peculiarly in her ears. Thomas reached out for her hand; Jake laughed cruelly. Britta cried, letting the tears fall on her chest. Nothing made sense; no one stayed long enough to explain. Only more blackness, and her head...it hurt all the time.

Finally the interminable darkness lifted, Reeta finding herself in the double bed that had been occupied by each of the measled children in turn. Though the room was dimly lit, her eyes closed involuntarily, preferring the darkness. She tried to speak, but her throat ached in the effort, only a dry rasping sound escaping her lips.

"Oh, thank God you are alive!" a voice cried at her side.

Reeta turned her head, straining to see who was there. Slowly the image came into focus. "Britta!" she mouthed the name painfully. But how could it be? The house must still be under quarantine. She didn't need to speak.

Britta immediately began pouring out her confession and along with it an explanation. "If you had died, I never could have forgiven myself," she wailed softly. "You have done nothing but good for me, and I, well. I lied to you. I stole the brooch on the train, and I spilled the ink on your dress on purpose, because I was jealous of you. It's my fault you are sick, too. I should have come that night. I only pretended that I wasn't feeling well. Can you forgive me at all?" she sobbed. "God, please forgive me!"

Moving her hand across the bed cover, Reeta rested it on top of Britta's icy arm. If only the room were warmer. Maybe then she could concentrate better. Britta's words bounced in and out, not making much sense.

"Here now. Let me put a damp towel on your forehead. You're still burning up with fever." She moved quietly across the room, returning to minister even as she had offered.

One thing Reeta did comprehend just then. Britta had broken the quarantine to take care of her. God was at work in the child's heart through no effort on Reeta's part. Foggily, the idea occurred to her that if Jake hadn't done what he did, she wouldn't have been here, and this change of heart might not have come about so soon.

Britta had brought a small light into the black room of Reeta's own bitterness. She could feel the dawn approaching. She welcomed it.

Chapter Twenty-Nine

MAIL BOAT

It was her friend, this stubby little boat that slipped into the dock each week. She knew her captain well. He was a crusty river man, his face wrinkled and tanned by constant exposure to the elements. Despite his tough appearance and the sharpness with which he addressed his crew, he was all politeness and decorum when it came to Reeta. Somehow Thomas had secured the promise of the old man to personally deliver his messages, which he did without fail.

"Ya, little miss," he said as he jumped from the boat to the dock, landing with a thud and a teasing grin. "You wouldn't be looking for something special, would you now?" He waved a cream-colored envelope addressed to one Reeta Juntunen of Astoria, Oregon.

She took the envelope knowing Thomas had parted with it only a short time ago. Did the old man know how wondrous it was to receive letters this way? Only the captain's hands touched the letters passed between the two of them. His weathered face smiling at both recipient and sender made the distance between them seem closer somehow.

How long had their letters been traveling like this? Fall had passed into a winter with little resemblance to the ones she had known in the white encrusted world of Puolanka. The snow hardly stayed long enough to tempt her with homesickness, soon making way for the fog and rain, which lasted far into spring. It was summer now.

Today she had even left her shawl at home, striding down to the wharf in great steps, her eyes taking in the changes the warmer days had brought. Slender green stalks had pushed through the cracks in the walkway, and Mrs. Rapaana's picket-fenced yard was all purple and yellow and red with flowers of every kind. Flowers made the house come alive. She reveled in the feeling, making a quick mental note to ask Thomas for some flower seed packets.

Remembering herself, Reeta handed over the letter she had brought for Thomas. "He is looking well?" she asked, hoping to hear something, anything about him.

Removing his cap respectfully, the old man scratched his balding head momentarily. He squinted at her in the bright afternoon sunlight, choosing his words carefully. "Well, them loggers keep mighty busy this time of year, you know. They all look plum worn out by the end of the week."

"Certainly," Reeta agreed. "But did he..." She didn't know quite how to ask what was on her mind. Many strange sicknesses plagued this new land. It wasn't that fear only, but the worry over accidents or injuries, too.

"Listen, child," he addressed her much as her own father would have. "These eyes may not be as good as they used to be, but he seemed fine to me. And if you don't mind me saying it, you are looking much better these days."

"Thank you," she said, blushing at his compliment. With the coming of the warm weather, she had felt the final release of the lingering symptoms from the measles. Slowly her body had regained its strength, the color of life coming back into her cheeks.

"Don't you worry none," the captain said, tucking the letter into the inside pocket of his coat. "I'll take good care of this." He made a half-bow, replacing his cap before he was off about his business.

Resisting the temptation to open the letter immediately, she clutched it tightly in her hand, retracing her steps up the hill toward the parsonage. Britta sat on the porch entertaining Anna, while bouncing baby Kaarina on her knee.

"Too warm in the house!" Anna announced, her nose wrinkled up quite comically. "Mother says we must stay outside and not get ourselves dirty. Some ladies are coming for coffee." She emphasized the word "ladies" with a flip of her skirt, revealing lacy undergarments.

"Such a lady you are!" Britta teased.

"Mother lets me sip coffee from her cup," Anna announced, this privilege not being allowed many three-year-olds.

"My, my!" Reeta marveled with due respect. "That is quite something." She exchanged glances with Britta, both of them barely able to muffle their laughter.

"Ah, what have you there?" Britta turned her teasing toward Reeta. "Another love letter? Do read it for us."

"Wouldn't you like that?" Reeta responded, blushing.

She stared at the same girl who, a few months earlier, had been so impossible. There was no other explanation for her marked change of temperament, except for her having settled her heart with God. She had even been spared from the measles, unlike Reeta, who had passed so near death.

"You'll have to excuse me, children," Reeta said, heading straight for her room. She deliberately postponed the pleasure of Thomas' letter a moment longer while she reclined comfortably across the pillows on her bed. One day his letter would say that the house was ready; he would be coming for her. Wishing would never make it so, but nevertheless, she hoped against hope that she would not have to stay a second winter in this city.

Suddenly she noticed another envelope propped up on the table beside her bed. The handwriting was the familiar elaborate script she herself had learned in school. There was no mistaking it; it was from Hanna. She did the writing, conveying family news along with her father's love and her mother's silence. Well, whatever the news from home, she would not let it spoil the letter from Thomas.

Perhaps it was her imagination, but his letter smelled like the forest, bark and pine. She could imagine exactly how he looked in his work clothes with those wide suspenders and clunky boots. He would be wearing the soft, gray wool coat that matched his eyes. She had saved enough money last winter to send it to him for Christmas.

Reading his letters, she frequently paused over words or reread some sentences several times, not wanting to come to the end. This letter brought more news of the house Thomas was having built for them. She couldn't quite imagine paying $800 for a house. Had her parents even seen that kind of money in their whole lives? She wondered. At the end of the letter, Thomas wrote of his longing for her. "I can only toil and work because it is for you, my dearest. The time of our separation will soon be past, and we will not be parted again."

She stared at the words. "How soon?" The question hung in the stuffy air of the upstairs room. Having devoured every word of his letter and still finding no clues, she folded it exactly along the original creases, slightly crooked, and placed it back in the envelope.

Then her attention turned toward the other letter. Might as well get all the news at once, she thought, opening the seal. Glancing at the signature first, she found that it was from Hanna, as she had expected.

> *Dear Sister,*
>
> *We all are praying that you are entirely well after your sickness. I don't know an easy way to tell you this, but as you know, Father has been getting on in years, though being quite sound in body. Last month he had a terrible accident in the woods. A log rolled onto his leg, crushing it badly. His leg never healed properly, and the spirit went out of him entirely...*

Tears clouded Reeta's eyes until she could read no farther. "Dear, sweet Father!" she murmured, blinking back the tears and wiping her damp cheeks. In a moment she was able to continue.

> *...We buried him today.*

The words glared at her from the page, their form growing and then shrinking back to normal size as some giant snake's tongue striking venom in her heart. She finished reading the letter, the words blending together, in a mournful dissidence until the last few paragraphs.

Though I haven't seen him, myself, there are rumors in Puolanka that Jake is back. He is supposed to be a ticket agent for some big mining company trying to recruit workers.

Mother says she misses you and the boys so much now, she doesn't know how she'll live, though I fear her pride is still keeping her from writing to you. Aatu sends his love. Pray for him. He has been doing poorly ever since his return.

Love,
Hanna

In the small attic room, which had suddenly grown cold, she lay on the bed crying until overcome by sleep. She had no idea how long she had lain there when gentle Aunt Kiki woke her. Learning of Reeta's sorrow, she began ministering comfort as only one of God's angels could. But even as the measles had drained her bodily strength, the news of her Father's passing and Aatu's poor health made her spirit ache. Strangely, the mention of Jake no longer stirred her anger, only her sympathy for the state of his soul.

* * *

Summer had nearly passed, when the black-garbed Reeta again appeared at the wharf. Britta had chiefly acted as letter carrier and intercessor, along with the captain, during the time of mourning. But this particular August afternoon, Reeta had not been able to resist the inclination to go herself.

However, the captain's typical greeting was absent, because of a great hubbub at the waterfront. Instead of the usual crowd gathered to gossip or buy fish, people were running about or pushing to get a look at something.

"It was an awful accident, they say."

"Indeed! The poor soul!"

"Who went for the doctor? Did anyone send for him?"

"Look out now!" bellowed the familiar commanding voice of the old captain. "Give the lad some room!"

Slowly the crowd backed away and Reeta squeezed in close enough to see between the shoulders of two bystanders. There lay the poor young man on a makeshift stretcher, his head wrapped round and round in rag bandages so she couldn't see the face. Then, suddenly, she caught her breath, not wanting to believe her eyes. A soft gray coat was tucked around him. The very coat she had sent Thomas last Christmas.

Chapter Thirty

PUOLANGAN HILLS

Reeta stood there, her feet frozen to the very spot. "Oh, God! Please...No!" was all she could pray.

Unnoticed by the crowd, she was pushed back as two young men from the boat took a position at each end of the stretcher, first carefully lifting the injured man, and then carrying him quickly away from her along the dock. The crowd followed, but she couldn't move.

"Oh, Miss, I'm sorry that you had to see such a sight," protested the captain. He came to her side, his face wrinkled in concern. "I didn't expect you'd come today. It's been so long, you know."

Reeta's gaze followed the procession heading up the street from the dock. "Thomas?" she finally managed to ask.

"Well, yes," the captain began, then correcting himself, as if realizing a mistake. "No, you don't understand."

She turned toward the captain at the same time a bearded young man carrying a small satchel hopped over the edge of the boat. They stared at each other in surprised recognition. He rushed to her, taking her up in a fierce embrace and whirling her around completely off the ground.

When at last Reeta had caught her breath, she spoke in amazement, "But the injured man. It was your coat."

"My coat?" Thomas repeated, not taking his eyes from her. "Oh, I gave it to keep the poor man warm. You didn't think..."

"What else was I to think?" she interrupted. "I couldn't live without you." She lowered her eyes, aware that the captain was still watching them.

Thomas took her hands, holding them firmly between his rough, blistered palms. "And I couldn't wait a day longer to come for you. The workers are finishing up on the main part of the house, and we should have time to get settled in before the rainy weather."

"Pardon me, sir," the captain said, looking nervously about, "but if you'll be going back up river, you and the young lady that is, be here Monday morning first thing." With that he bowed and was off up the dock to check on the injured man.

Thomas picked up the satchel he had dropped, easing it over one shoulder. With the other hand, he gathered her close to his side, leading her along the walkway

"You didn't tell me about the beard," she commented, reaching out to touch the silky brown fullness.

"Wasn't certain you'd like the idea," he said apologetically. "Meant to shave it off before I came, but I kind of got attached to it."

"It makes you look older," she stated simply.

"I am older."

"And I, too."

They stopped for a moment to consider each other. It had been three years since the evening Thomas had told her of his love. She touched his forehead softly, tracing the lines etched there by hard work. His eyes bore no boyish crush, but a devoted resolution to love her always.

She, in her black mourning dress, had changed from the stubborn schoolgirl, who didn't know what she wanted, into a woman. This woman standing beside him had waited and trusted, even suffering the pangs of separation, illness, and death. Yet she was his. Though neither of them would have chosen the path they had come, the very trials that had kept them apart now cast a firm cord around them, binding them together as nothing else might have.

Little was spoken as they walked up the street to the parsonage. It was almost too much to believe, she thought. Just the feel of his arm around her was enough for now. He, too, was lost in his own thoughts, not needing to speak.

When Britta caught sight of them, however, the scene changed rapidly. She let out a raucous whoop before running into the house to tell everyone the news. Before they reached the porch, Aunt Kiki, Rev. Rosberg, and all the children came streaming down the steps. After all the hugging and jumping up and down (that being the children's part mainly) was done, they sat on the porch while Thomas was interrogated thoroughly. Only when past, present, and future plans had been described in detail, did Aunt Kiki consent to retreating to the kitchen to begin supper.

Since it had been too short notice to properly prepare the cabin in the wood, that evening and the one to follow, Reeta and Thomas shared the small attic room that had been home for her since arriving in Astoria.

"How strange to have you here, right here beside me," she whispered when they were alone that night. "I've hoped for this day for so long, but I still can't believe it."

He pulled her closer underneath the warm coverlets, whispering in her ear, "I feel like crying with joy myself." Then in a quivering voice, barely in control of himself, he prayed softly, still speaking into her ear. "Lord, Your ways are perfect; Your paths are good. Thank you for taking care of Reeta and keeping her for me. Thank you for providing a place for us together in this world. May our lives be pleasing to You, Father. Amen and amen." He kissed her again and again, never releasing her from his embrace until dawn was nearly ready to break across the velvet sky.

Before Thomas awoke, she slipped out of bed to wash and dress. Then tiptoeing across the room with a breakfast tray she had prepared herself, she called softly, "Thomas, my dear, time to be up."

He squinted at her through sleepy eyes, and then smiled while reaching out to grab her.

"Now, now, none of that," she warned. "It's a beautiful Lord's Day, and we must be off to church soon. I want everyone to see such a fine husband has come for me. There are so many good-byes that need to be said this day." She set the tray on the bed, but he only looked at her strangely.

"Your mourning clothes," he said as though he had figured out some mysterious puzzle. "That's what's different about you. You are beautiful."

She stood before him dressed in her Sunday dress of dark green to match her eyes. She blushed at his compliment, explaining, "It didn't seem right to wear black today. I'm sure Father would understand, don't you think?"

He nodded, still admiring her. "I'm sure he would," he said, not seeming surprised at her decision. "That's my Reeta."

Many heads were turned, some completely out of joint it seemed, at church that morning when they arrived with the pastor and his wife. The few old women, outraged by Reeta's impropriety, were far outnumbered by the well-wishers and friends. It was wonderful to see her looking so well, they said, and how good to see the bridegroom again. Little else was talked about that morning before the service.

Sitting together on the hardwood bench beside a glowing Britta and the rest of the Rosberg family, Thomas squeezed Reeta's hand. "This is one thing we'll not have for a while, a church building that is. But before the little ones start coming, I'll wager it will be built." He winked at her and rolled his eyes.

She blushed almost as crimson as the hymnal, while Britta begged, "What did he say? Tell me!"

The rest of the day was spent packing and sorting through the gifts that had been showered on them for their new home. Aunt Kiki and Britta had somehow secretly made a lovely patchwork quilt. It was their first thoroughly American present. If only they had a bed to put it on, Thomas had joked.

It was a foggy dawn the next day when Rev. Rosberg helped load their things in the wagon to drive them to the wharf. Aunt Kiki cried, as did Britta.

"Please, don't," protested Reeta, "or I shall be crying, too, and on the happiest day of my life."

They both obediently dried their tears. "You must write and tell us everything," Britta said, giving Reeta a hug. "And you take care of her," she warned, shaking her finger in Thomas' face.

By the time the fog had burned off, revealing the thickly forested trees along the northern shoreline, the boat had taken them far upriver. Occasionally a passing vessel would sound its horn, but the drone of the small engine and the rhythmic thumping of the waves against the bow were the background for the quiet conversation floating between the passengers.

Before noon they pulled into the dock at Stella, the place Reeta had only imagined from Thomas' description. A store and postal station had been built on the very edge of the river. Across the street, built right against a steep hillside, was a church, its doors facing the river as if to welcome anyone going by. A few smaller buildings were scattered nearby, and a group of congenial loggers lounged about.

"There!" Thomas pointed. "There's our wagon. I'll see that the team gets hitched up while you start loading your things." He patted her hand and was gone.

Bidding good-bye to the captain, Reeta was certain even he held back a few tears. Then they began the long ride over the hills on deeply-rutted dirt roads. Thomas ate ravenously from the lunch Aunt Kiki had packed, but Reeta was too excited.

"This is the long way to get to our place," Thomas explained, "and from now on we'll do most of our trading in Catlin or Kelso, right along the Cowlitz River."

She couldn't quite comprehend the geography of it all, but it mattered little. Their home was only over a few more hills. The sun had painted the sky all pink and blue by the time the wagon turned onto a lane with slender maple trees on each side. Reeta stared in wonder at the trees, stretching their branches over the road as if to form a bridal bower.

"We're almost home," Thomas spoke in reverent awe. "Did I tell you this place has been called the 'Puolangan Hills' because so many from our village have settled here?"

She couldn't reply, but clung to his sleeve as the wagon came to the crest of the hill, and there, nestled in a small green valley, stood the house, freshly shingled and ready. Its porch shaded the front windows like a hand held over a person's eyes, watching for them.

"Oh, Thomas, it's perfect!" she marveled. "Father would have been so proud of you." She turned to look at his face. Lines of contentment were etched in the profile. "Thomas Juntunen," she whispered, no trace of doubt in her voice, "Do you know that I love you?"

The house on Columbia Heights,
a.k.a. The Puolangan Hills.

AFTERWARD

Though many of the characters in this story bear their true names and were actual people, this is a work of fiction, and being such, is not intended to be a factual account. The truth is that the main characters did come to Columbia Heights, a place known by the Finns as the Puolongan Hills, above the Longview/Kelso area in Washington. Happenings in Finland, at Ellis Island, and in Astoria very *loosely* follow the basic facts of Reeta's life. Thomas did have a twin who remained in Finland, and to whom I apologize for making him the villain of the story.

The factual account of the lives of Thomas and Reeta Juntunen was written by Carolyn Caines and was published in the *Cowlitz Historical Quarterly* in Volume 52, Number 4, December 2010. The article was entitled, "Sisu Defined Grandparents' Generation." It is available at:

COWLITZ COUNTY HISTORICAL MUSEUM
405 Allen Street
Kelso, WA 98626
phone: 360-577-3119
website: www.co.cowlitz.wa.us/museum

ABOUT THE AUTHOR

Carolyn Caines is a third-generation resident of Southwest Washington State. She and her husband Michael have three married children and seven grandchildren.

During her college years, she wrote and published a dozen short stories. A graduate of Seattle Pacific College, she taught grades K-4 and high school English for thirty years.

Carolyn began writing this story more than twenty years ago as part of a writing class, but put the book project aside after making a few copies for family.

In the last fifteen years, Carolyn has been a successful poet, having published more than 130 poems in various magazines and journals. She recently published her first book of poetry, *IN THE NOISELESS NIGHT*, and since 1998, she continues to write a weekly e-mailing called *Poems For You*.

You may contact her through her website:
www.carolyncaines.com